EMERALD ISLE OF MISTS

THE MAGIC OF INHERIAN: BOOK 3

TERRY SPEAR

SYNOPSIS

Prince Argon has taken Lady Kersta and her companions hostage because he needs them to help him rescue his sister from captivity and then he must return to his princedom and make his twin brother pay for his crimes. Kersta and her friends have special abilities that he hopes to use. But now they have a new problem. The prince's sister is being offered to either one of two suitors, and they're in the fight to the death to keep her. The man who holds the strings is a king who claims she's his niece, but Argon knows the man is not their uncle!

Kersta can't believe she and her companions have paid passage on the prince's ship to take them home and instead he's taken them to the Emerald Isle of Mists on a rescue mission and all because a soothsayer has predicted this will come to pass. Not only is danger all around them, but Kersta's whole life is about to be turned upside down.

Thanks so much for reading all my different genres, Gail Dockery. I'm dedicating this book to you and yes, it will be in print! I love my print readers! May your journey always take you to a happily ever after!

http://www.terryspear.com/

Print ISBN: 978-1-63311-081-6

Ebook ISBN: 978-1-63311-080-9

1

On board the sailing ship the Duchess that was supposed to be taking Lady Kersta and her companions home from Albion to Inherian, Kersta hoped nothing went wrong. But she had an uneasy feeling something wasn't quite right. She'd been attempting to read the sailors' minds and hadn't gleaned anything. Her "talent" was so new to her that she used it every chance she got, especially when she wanted to make sure she and her friends weren't putting themselves at some risk. The sailors had busied themselves with sailing the ship for the last couple of days and deliberately seemed to avoid thinking of anything important whenever she was around like when she and her companions had boarded the ship or when crewmembers brought them their meals. Which seemed odd.

People thought about things all the time, concerns, what they had just been doing, what they had to do next, what had happened in the distant past. It was unnatural for so many crewmembers not to be thinking about something. Just...anything.

None here but her companions even knew about her ability

to read minds though, so she couldn't imagine why they would purposefully hide their thoughts from her. If they were. Unless they were being controlled by a mage so that they couldn't give away their thoughts, or their thoughts were no longer their own. She and her friends had dealt with so many strange, fantastical, and dangerous issues, she couldn't be sure about anything.

In the captain's quarters, she sat down with Princess Talamaya and Lady Mexia, a mage, all three of them from the Kingdom of Damar, and Gallant, a dwarf adventurer from the village of Kern. But Kersta knew something wasn't right.

Her brow wrinkled deep in thought, the princess also seemed concerned. Like the rest of them, strands of her dark brown hair, only somewhat lighter than the others, and streaked by the sun, had loosened from some of her braids pinned close to her head.

"What puzzles you, princess?" Kersta asked her. "Have you had a vision?"

Talamaya turned to consider Kersta, her dark brown eyes darker than normal. "Yes, but I don't know what to make of it. It should take us no more than two days' sailing time to reach our destination of the continent of Inherian, and yet, I have had a vision that we'll land somewhere else. A verdant green island, it appears, cloaked in mists."

"Perhaps King Lazarion intends to take you on a trip there, following your wedding," Mexia offered, trying to lighten the serious mood. "Before you settle in Malaron with him."

The dwarf Gallant, tugged at his dark brown beard, braided down to his waist, his bushy brows bridging his thick nose, wrinkled with distress. His black beady eyes darted from Kersta to the princess. Princess Talamaya had saved his life and he swore a debt of gratitude to her, though he'd saved her life also. Kersta knew he wanted to stay with them, as many adventures as they seemed to be having during their travels.

"Are ye sure your vision is correct, woman?" Gallant asked.

Princess Talamaya nodded. "They always come to pass. Though I cannot tell everything I would like to from them or when the visions will actually occur."

Kersta poked her fork into her dish of Caledonia fish. "I don't understand why the captain has our meal served in his quarters, but never eats with us. Don't you think it odd?"

"Perhaps he is afraid of his men getting too close to us women," Mexia offered. "Maybe he feels if he sups with us, they'll be jealous. They had leered at us once we boarded as if *we* were the main course for dinner." She tilted her small chin up, waiting for Kersta to agree. Her brown hair was darker than the princess's. And her almond-shaped eyes, the same color, sparkled in the flicker of the lanterns' lights. Straggles of hair swept across her cheeks, lightly moistened from the cool dampness of the room.

Fingering her brown bread, Kersta nodded. Yet...the crewmembers didn't think about *anything*, even when they had cast a glance their way and might have had lecherous thoughts. "We have paid good money for our passage. I do not like it that the captain doesn't wish for us to walk on his decks even for one brief moment. On the ship we took to the continent of Albion, we had no such trouble. The captain allowed us free movement. I cannot stand to be hemmed in always."

"He doesn't want us to get in the way of his men," Mexia explained. "These sailors seem unrulier than the ones on the other ship. We've heard them fighting on the decks, seen them shoving each other before the bos'n mate took them to task."

Kersta raised a brow at her. "And the captain hasn't even welcomed us, his passengers, aboard yet. We have already been on his ship for what? Two days? Which should have been the duration of our journey. And who's that man who hides beneath a cloak and appeared on deck when we first came aboard? He's an odd one, that one."

"I think Mexia's right. Some of the men appear to be the sort who need close supervision, or the work will not get done. As to the cloaked man, I agree, and I don't trust him in the least bit." The princess took a bite of her fish.

"He is the one who bought us wine at the Dragon's Keep Tavern in Langdon," Mexia said. "I recognize his cloak. Though it appears only to be a dull common type of brown wool, heavy enough to keep out the rain and cold, there's something regal about it."

"You're so right. The clasp." Kersta looked up at her companions to see them watching her. "It's gold. Nothing common about that. And it's inlaid with a green gem...emerald possibly. Plus, to pay for passage on the ship, he must have had some money."

"Hmm, and I still wonder why he paid for our drinks at the tavern," the princess said. "If the mages hadn't begun a barroom brawl with the soldiers and pirates, maybe he would have spoken to us."

"Instead, he slipped out during the fight, like a man afraid of his own shadow." Mexia lifted another spoonful of soup to her lips. "Not heroic in the least."

"Maybe he is not trained in the art of fighting." Kersta ate some of her smoked cheese.

The princess tapped her long fingernails on the captain's oak dining table, with room to seat eight comfortably. "If he is a passenger like us, why does he not eat with us?"

"I told you then, and I tell you now, he's fighting demons in his head. He's not one to be trusted." Kersta buttered another slice of bread. Then she sipped from her flask filled with healing tea the soothsayer, Modi, provided each of the ladies for their initial journey, ever replenishing.

Kersta suddenly felt strange and rose from her well-worn,

wooden chair, slightly disoriented, her head spinning along with her stomach. "Can you use your mage magic, Mexia?"

Mexia frowned at her. "Whatever is the matter?"

"I just feel funny. Lightheaded." Kersta looked down at the griffin soup she'd supped from.

"What do you want me to do?" Mexia continued frowning at her, as if she hadn't been affected by whatever ailed Kersta.

"Anything. Just see if your magic works. I...I think something in the soup affected me. Poison? Can you use your magic here?"

Mexia made Kersta's chair levitate, then she rested it on the wooden floor again. "My magic seems to be intact."

"Can you transport us back to the seaport city of Langdon?" Kersta tried to keep her voice calm, but her words were already tinged with panic. Though she was relieved Mexia's magic was working. "Don't eat any more of the food, just in case it has been...drugged."

"Are you certain you want me to transport us? I can only transport two of you at a time. And even then, I don't know if I can from that far away. What if being separated from the land by water interfered? I could drown us," Mexia said.

"Can you take us back in time, then?" Kersta clutched the back of her chair, trying to still her reeling thoughts.

"For what purpose?" Mexia asked, sounding puzzled.

Kersta collapsed on her chair, the panic rising in her blood. "My thoughts are growing muddled. Are not yours?"

They glanced over at Gallant whose head rested on the table already. A snore escaped his lips.

The princess touched her temple. "We've been drugged, I fear. Like you, my thoughts are becoming disoriented. I cannot see anything in the future and I'm having a difficult time holding onto the present."

Mexia rose unsteadily to her feet, then made her way to the door, nearly falling twice with the rocking of the ship. When she reached the knob, she twisted but found resistance. "Orc's dung! They've locked us in."

Kersta rubbed her temple, attempting to clear her mind. "They are taking us to the islands locked in mists, do you not think? Your vision, Princess. It is not in the distant future but now."

"Why?" Mexia slipped to the floor in a heap of blue gowns.

"I don't know. The vision that Talamaya had. It has to be. What else can you do, Mexia?"

"Stop time." Mexia raised her hands to cast the spell, then dropped them into her lap, closed her eyes, and fell asleep.

Kersta groaned. "Mexia." She glanced over at the princess slumped over in her seat, her head resting beside her bowl of soup, sound asleep. Then, despite her struggles to keep her mind awake and alert, Kersta gave in to the overwhelming need to sleep too.

KERSTA WOKE to the sound of someone rustling through papers on the captain's desk. Her head pounded still from the effects of the drug. Through heavily lidded eyes, she watched the man rifle through the papers. Then he turned his head toward her. She shut her eyes, but not before she'd had a look at him.

Blue eyes, troubled, dark as a stormy sea. Furrowed dark blond brows knit together as he scowled. Wisps of blond hair loosened from a leather-bound ponytail met his broad shoulders that seemed to carry the whole weight of the world upon them. She took a deep breath to curb the anxiety worming its way into the pit of her stomach. He wore the woolen cloak fastened with the emerald clasp. He was the only other passenger on the boat...or was he a passenger at all?

"Ahhh," he said, and she chanced to peek at him again. "Here 'tis."

He studied the document, then slid it under his cloak.

Who was he after all, and what did he want with them?

She turned to see if any of her companions stirred. None. They all slept the sleep of the dead. Mexia's mage powers would come in handy about now.

"You are awake," he said.

Kersta whipped her head around to see him watching her, a brow arched in amusement, an almost smile curving his lips.

"Who are you?"

"Argon," he said, with a low bow as if she were royalty, which she was. Yet the way he knew how to make the courtly gesture made her believe he had to be part of a court. His tone was gentile.

"Why are we here? Why were we drugged?" Kersta was trying to keep the furor out of her voice since the man seemed to have them under his control—for the moment.

"I need your services."

"Ours? You couldn't have asked us?"

"You were going home. I couldn't risk that you would turn me down. Not with the special...talents all of you have. I need you. You do something for me, and I'll take you to your home in Inherian."

"We paid for passage!" Kersta was furious with the man. "Are you the captain? I want to speak to the captain."

"I am the owner of this sailing ship, the captain, and your captor. You will do what I ask of you. You must. You have a great stake in it also."

Kersta shakily stood, still feeling the aftereffects of the drug, grabbing a post to steady herself. "What stake is that?" She didn't believe it for a moment. He was just using them.

"You will find the man of your dreams on this quest, so says the soothsayer I've spoken to."

"Oh really." She didn't believe him. He'd taken them away from their destination after they'd paid good money for the transportation, drugged them, and now was forcing them to do a quest for him?

"You have no choice in the matter. We'll be setting ashore on the Emerald Isle of Mists soon. And you and your companions will help me in my quest."

The Emerald Isle of Mists—of legends of beasts and who knew what else lurked in the forests, lakes, and along the coast. She'd heard there was even a castle in the middle of the island, but no one she'd ever known had actually been there.

Since she didn't have much choice in the matter, Kersta asked, "So what is this quest?"

"My brother has stolen my lands, my castle, and the treasury."

"You are a prince? Or a king?"

"Prince."

"What if your brother is a better leader than you? Wouldn't we be doing a disservice to your people? Just because you inherited the title and position, doesn't mean you are worthy of having it." Kersta had seen that before in other kingdoms.

Argon cast her a small, amused smile. "Okay, I agree. So you'll have to trust me that my brother is ruthless. He has already stolen my inheritance. He actually had his friends attempt to assassinate me, but I managed to escape. I believe he has sent our sister to the Emerald Isle of Mists. I must free her and return her home and vanquish my brother forever.

"I've been watching the three of you ladies, listening to the stories regaling us with your conquests, hearing about your abilities. Rumors abound that you can fight great battles, defeat monsters that others succumb to, and come out with barely a scratch. You're intelligent, combat ready, and have your powers. I need your help."

In other words? He couldn't fight his way out of a burlap sack, and he needed three women and a dwarf to win his battles for him? "What do you think we can do about it?"

"The solution is on the Emerald Isle of Mists, once we free my sister. So says the soothsayer, Modi."

"Truly?" Modi had given Kersta and her friends the replenishing tea that they drank on their journey. It healed them, but also their waterskins never ran dry. Modi had made their staffs into lethal weapons, but also added a way to put their enemies to sleep for a time. If Modi told Argon that they would free his sister and find the solution to ousting his twin brother from ruling his princedom, he would be able to do so.

"Aye, and"—he took a deep breath and let it out—"Modi says you will find your husband."

2

Prince Argon wanted to get the answers he needed right away before his twin brother could eliminate him as he had wanted to do. It wasn't enough that Zane had stolen his property while Argon was trying to negotiate a peace treaty with another realm, but then to learn his sister had vanished? And Zane had wanted Argon dead, afraid he would return and take his princedom back. Zane didn't care that Mirabella was lost to them and could be in grave danger herself. And Argon suspected Zane was the reason their sister had disappeared and ended up on the Emerald Isle of Mists. Not only that, Argon wondered if the hunting accident that had caused their father's death hadn't been an accident after all.

Argon let out his breath and spread his hands out, palms up, beseeching Kersta to help him to locate his sister first, and then he would take Kersta and her companions home to Inherian. Though if Modi was right, Kersta and he would be taking this whole business in a different direction. But he didn't want to bring that up just yet.

"My sister, Mirabella, vanished and I have searched for her everywhere, buying information where I could. That's when I began hearing that she had been taken to the Emerald Isle of Mists. Then I found the soothsayer, the same one that you had seen. She verified for me that my sister was indeed being held captive there. At the same time, I had learned of all your feats. Modi said our quests were interwoven as one. Without you, I would not succeed. Without me, you would not either. With your help, I'm hoping we can find Mirabella and rescue her. I fear she is in the worst sort of danger. I will return you to Inherian while I pursue a way to take the crown back. But I need your help in securing my sister's safety. That's what matters the most."

He had been so certain the women wouldn't help him. They were made adventurer guild members in one of the villages on the continent of Albion, which meant they could hire out to solve quests. But Princess Talamaya had royal duties that she no doubt had to attend to back at her castle before she joined her betrothed, the barbarian king Lazarion, after having recovered the scepter of salvation. Lady Mexia had only left with her companions because she wanted to be mage school trained, and they wanted to see her safely there. Now she would want to return to her betrothed, Derek, also a mage, once she took care of business in Inherian.

He had hoped Kersta would believe him when he told her she would find the man she would marry on the island—a soothsayer was never wrong—but he could understand how she wouldn't trust him after he had stolen her and her companions away. Though she'd intrigued him from the first time he'd laid eyes on her while on their quests.

He had hoped to leave the dwarf behind, but Gallant hadn't been about to be separated from the women and so Argon had to let him come along for the ride and hoped he didn't have to fight him. Gallant might not have any magical abilities, but he was a well-trained fighter.

"Okay, so we go along with your plan since we have no other choice. But you will have to make it worth our while. We are part of a guild and will be paid handsomely for our endeavor," Kersta said.

"Freeing an innocent woman is not enough?" the prince asked, though he would pay the women and Gallant any amount of money to help him free his sister.

"Freeing what innocent woman?" Talamaya asked, rubbing her forehead as she stirred, but couldn't seem to quite focus her eyes on anything yet.

Argon had regretted having to put the companions to sleep. He had hoped they would have offered to do what was right. They had done so on all their other quests. He explained their quest.

"You couldn't just have asked us for our assistance?" Talamaya asked, sounding perturbed.

Kersta folded her arms. "He is paying us a mountain of gold to save his sister."

Talamaya smiled.

Argon didn't want to remind them he had no access to his mountains of gold without ousting his brother from their princedom first.

Someone knocked on the door and Argon said, "Come."

The bos'n mate opened the door and peered in. "We are ready to launch the transport boat, Captain."

"Aye, we'll board now."

Halton glanced at the sleeping mage and dwarf.

"Have some men carry them to the transport boat," Argon said. They could wake up on the shore and then they would head into the interior of the island to reach the castle where he presumed his sister was being held captive.

"Aye-aye, Captain."

Halton closed the door and moments later returned with

men ready to carry out Argon's orders. One of them helped Princess Talamaya to her feet and the two of them left the captain's quarters. The men carried the sleeping companions out next.

"Are you going with us?" Kersta asked Argon.

"Aye. She is my sister, and if I have to, I will die trying to free her."

Kersta scoffed and left the cabin with him. "Then we will not be paid our mountain of gold." Then she frowned at him. "How are your crew and you able to hide your thoughts from me? Is the ship cloaked in magic, or do you have a mage aboard unbeknownst to us?"

Argon smiled a little at her. "You are not the only ones with some innate magic abilities. I can hide people's thoughts from others who might be able to access them. Not from any distance, but aboard the ship or while traveling, I can do so."

"Oh." She walked with him across the upper deck toward the transport boat. "Well, don't hide my friends' thoughts from me. It aids me in working with them on quests."

He arched a brow. He was certain she wanted to know their thoughts for more than that reason.

She saw his expression of disbelief and her face turned a little red. She quickly brushed a lock of hair out of her eyes. "That is all. Do you...do you read minds?"

"No. I can only conceal others' thoughts."

She sighed with audible relief.

He chuckled. "You like to know other's thoughts but don't wish your own to be known."

"Aye. It gives me the advantage. Sometimes."

Then the men helped Kersta into the transport boat and Argon joined her. Some of the men had already loaded his bags and the companions' into the vessel. Six men manned the oars as others lowered the boat into the water.

And then as soon as it settled into the choppy water, they began rowing to the shore.

"We...we are not at the seaport of our home." Mexia rubbed the sleep from her eyes, peering at the island cloaked in mists.

"No, this is the Emerald Isle of Mists. We have a new quest to fulfill, it seems," Princess Talamaya said.

Argon explained the mission.

"A mountain of gold? Just how big is the mountain?" Mexia asked.

The ladies all looked at Argon to see what he had to say.

"As much as you would like, if we're able to free my sister and safely return her to the ship."

Talamaya sighed. "We must always fulfill our quests by seeking the right path. If that means doing it for naught but the satisfaction that we have freed your sister, that will be what must be."

Gallant stirred from his sleep. "Maybe for you, woman, but 'tis a bounty I'm seeking. I canna live off the generosity of the peoples of our world."

"Did you hear what our quest is?" Kersta asked him.

Gallant stroked his beard. "Aye. A fight to the death, nay doubt, though we will succeed when they will not."

"Who?" Talamaya asked.

Gallant raised his war hammer toward the beach. "Unless those three men are a welcoming committee, I assume we have to fight them. Ren and I are ready."

"Ren is the name of his war hammer," Kersta explained to Argon.

That's when they could see a parting of the mists and three men pacing along the beach, waiting for them, unarmed, appearing harmless, but they must have heard the rowing of the boat, the water slapping at the sides, maybe even their conversation and they were prepared to meet them. All three men had handsome features, almost uncommonly so.

"I've never heard of anything that was welcoming here in the stories I've been told," Argon said.

"They look harmless, but I see in their thoughts they are the two-faced kishi," Kersta warned. "They welcome the unsuspecting, then once you accept their greeting and greet them in return, they turn their face around and devour you with a head that is like that of a hyena. Once they lock you in their jaws, there is no escape. They are waiting for their nooning meal. They're practically salivating with the prospect we will be it."

Argon was indeed glad Kersta was assisting him in this quest. Like she said, they appeared harmless, no weapons on hand. He normally wouldn't have initiated a fight with unarmed men.

"How do you want to handle this?" Gallant gripped his battle hammer with resolve. "I canna fight them until we are on the shore."

"We cannot strike them with our deadly staffs until we are standing on the shore either." Talamaya frowned at Argon. "Are your men going to assist in the battle, Argon?"

Argon shook his head. "If we were to lose my ship's crew, we would not be able to return to the ship, nor sail away once we have my sister in hand."

"Must we fight fair?" Mexia asked.

"Nay," Gallant quickly said before anyone had a chance to say yes. "They wouldna give us a fair chance. They are two-faced, dinna you see?"

"All right. If Talamaya agrees, I will use my magic. Um, can the kishi swim?" Mexia asked Kersta.

"Aye. They are basically two-faced men. So if they have learned to swim, they can swim," Kersta said.

"Oh, so if I levitate them over the sea and drop them in, they still can come after us." Mexia sounded disheartened by the notion.

"Aye," Talamaya said, "but it is the right thing to do. Send them far enough out to sea that they will never reach us in time. Send them to the leeward side of the island far out to sea and they won't give the sailors any difficulty either."

Mexia raised her arms in the rocking boat, her fingers ready to take care of the menace before them. "I can only do two at a time. When the remaining kishi sees that his companions are flying through the air, he'll probably run away, and we might have to deal with him later."

"And the other two as well once they swim ashore," Kersta said.

"Do you read their thoughts?" Talamaya asked.

"They think Mexia is bluffing that she can do anything to them." Kersta smiled. "Do your worst, Mexia."

"Take care of the two biggest men first," Talamaya said, "though wiry men can be more agile and quicker on their feet."

Mexia lifted the two most muscular men and carried them over the island until none of them could see where the men would land. "Um, I have a problem."

"Aye?" Talamaya asked.

"I can't see the ocean. The island is surrounded by mists."

The men in her mage's grasp wiggled to be free of her spell, screaming to the other kishi to attack the mage in the transport boat. The remaining man watched his friends as if he was under a different kind of spell, unable to move, his mouth agape, his hyena's head looking down at the sand while his human head was focused on his friends high up in the blue, cloudless sky.

"How far should I go?" Mexia sounded tired, like she couldn't hold onto them for very much longer.

"Hold on for as long as you can," Talamaya said.

Argon was thinking that if Mexia dropped them too far out

to sea, they might never make it back to shore. If she was unable to move them beyond the island and she dropped them from too far up, that could be the end of them as they fell back to the land. Either worked for him because once they freed his sister, the fewer the number of monsters they had to face, the better.

Then Mexia released the kishi and turned her attention to the remaining man. He didn't run off like they thought he would. He dove into the water, Argon readied his sword, Gallant nearly tipping them over as he moved to strike the kishi with his hammer. Before they capsized the boat, Mexia lifted the kishi out of the sea, dripping wet, still stroking with his arms and kicking with his feet as if he were in the water. She carried him far away over the island.

Argon could see mountains and he wondered just how far away the castle was that most likely held his sister hostage. He suspected his brother had paid someone to bring her here. Though journeying through the forests and jungles and swamps and whatever else they might face meant whoever had brought her here knew how to navigate it safely. At least he hoped so for Mirabella's sake.

His men rowed onto the beach and quickly helped the ladies out of the transport. Gallant sank to his chin in the warm, salty water, whereas when Aragon stepped into the water, it was only knee deep.

"Row the transport back to the Duchess. We'll send word when we need to be picked up," Argon said to his men. They would be safer on the ship while waiting for his return.

"Aye, Captain," several of the men said, sounding eager to return to the safety of the ship after offloading the party's bags.

"Do you have a map of this place?" Kersta asked Argon.

He smiled at her. "Did you read my mind?"

"For once you were not blocking my reading of your thoughts. But the map doesn't show where the castle is exactly.

You suspect it is in the center of the island, away from the storms that plague the isle. Though we are lucky we are here on a clear day." Kersta held her hand out for the map.

He pulled it out of his shirt, and they spread it on the sandy beach to decide which way to go. He was used to being in charge of all decisions. But he needed their help, and he would share what all he knew, which was very little. "I believe my brother hired someone to bring my sister here."

"She is in the castle, the northern most tower of the keep," Talamaya said. "I can see her looking out the window, hoping to catch a glimpse of a way to escape."

"Then she is like us, unwilling to let her fate be sealed by another," Mexia said.

"Which way should we go?" Gallant was squinting hard at the map.

"Do you need spectacles to read it, Gallant?" Kersta asked.

Gallant turned to frown at her. "You will find your husband on this quest, so says the soothsayer. I am thankful 'tis no' me."

Kersta stared at him. "Argon shared that with me while you were asleep."

Gallant peered back down at the map.

"Gallant, how do you know this?" Kersta asked.

"I woke for a brief moment, heard what Argon said to you, and drifted back to sleep. What? Do ye think I have magical powers like the lot of you and have been holding out on you? Och, woman, ye try my patience."

"As if you ever had any," Kersta said.

"When you learned about this place, you must have had a notion of which way you would go first," Talamaya said to Argon.

"Aye. That way. I don't know if it's the safest or if it will get us where we're going the quickest, but see here"—he pointed to mounds of what looked like sand surrounded by water—"this appears to be quicksand. At least I think so. And here is a thick forest, so we'd have the cover of the trees. Here is a meadow, seems peaceful, but no telling what we would find there."

"Or in the woods," Mexia said. "We've encountered many a dark creature living in forests."

"Aye. And here the mountains are with one path through them. I believe any path could be treacherous. We just need to decide how we want to go first," Argon said, not about to pretend he knew best. "The person who sold me the map may have made it up, for all I know."

Kersta threw her hands up in the air. "Now you tell us."

"That's why I didn't show you the map right away. If my brother knew where I'd been searching for our sister, he might have paid this 'helpful' soul to give me the map of the isle."

"That no one has seen and lived to tell the tale concerning?" Talamaya asked.

"Wait, what if your sister isn't even here? That you undertook this journey for naught, but could easily perish for your efforts?" Kersta asked.

"Modi said she would be," Argon said.

"Aye, I see her in a tower. Blond like you? Right, Argon?" Talamaya said. "So some of it is true."

"Aye," Argon said.

"The man who said she was on the isle was the same man who sold you the map?" Kersta asked.

"Aye."

"How did *he* come by the map?" Kersta asked as Gallant began to walk toward the forest.

Argon watched Gallant, ready to come to his aid if something jumped out of the woods to fight him. "He said a man was dying and told him one day a man would come to purchase it, a prince on a great quest, and to sell it to no one else."

Talamaya looked up from the map and watched Gallant

close in on the forest. "We go Gallant's way. I suspect it is as good or as bad as any other."

They all headed after Gallant, though Mexia glanced at Kersta and said, "Who is this man you shall find on this quest who will be your husband?"

"It is not Gallant." Kersta was adamant about that.

Talamaya and Mexia both laughed.

"Ye laugh, but she would be lucky to have me," Gallant grumbled.

But then their attention was on the woods in front of them. All were concerned they would be facing perils unforetold at any time.

3

Princess Mirabella stopped pacing and turned to look at the window of the tower castle, not sure what had made her look. Nothing had ever happened out the window, yet she had a strong feeling that she needed to turn and look. Startling her, she gasped to see a tall ship—one of her brother's ships—Argon's Duchess anchored in the sea. Her brother had found her.

Or at least he was on his way to finding her. She adored Argon. He was the perfect choice to lead their people. She hadn't thought she'd ever see him again, not when she'd over-heard Zane talking to his second-in-command about hiring an assassin to kill Argon.

Mirabella leaned way out the window of the fourth floor of the circular tower at Mayen Castle, wishing she could fly away like the eagles and hawks that soared high above Larimar Forest. She wished she could steal a horse and ride unnoticed through the Grand'Mere Pass. That she could slip away into the dense forests and high mountains to the beach where her brother was no doubt landing.

What lay beyond the Five Sisters of Xerxes, the mountains

that dominated the northern sky? What lay west beyond Larimar Forest? And east? She'd heard savages lived there by the sea, bloodthirsty pirates who took everything they could carry away, and two-faced kishi—beautiful faces until they turned their head and their victims saw their vicious hyena's faces and felt their teeth before the kishi killed them.

She sighed. There were no bars to keep Mirabella from escaping the tower, but the drop would kill her and there was no way to climb down that she could see.

She prayed her brother had brought enough men to fight whatever monsters lurked on the island. She knew she couldn't fight the guards inside the tower to make her escape without a lot of aid.

She hadn't even been able to tell her brother that she'd witnessed Zane murdering their father on a hunt. No one who was involved in the hunting 'accident' that day knew she had seen what had happened. Only she suspected her brother Zane had seen her witness it, which was why he must have paid to have her brought here against her will. She guessed he at least couldn't handle the idea of having her eliminated, though being held here as a prisoner for the rest of her life could be worse. She wanted to avenge her father's death and help Argon take over the rule of their people. What if he failed to rescue her? She would lose her beloved brother and be stuck here forever.

Then she heard the sound of footfalls approaching her tower chamber and Mirabella quickly looked at the door. A key was inserted in the lock in the door, and she folded her arms.

Once Zane had taken over, he ruled with an iron fist, commanding all to bow to his whim.

But *her*. He could never rule *her*. And somehow, as the gods were her witnesses, she'd return and free her people from Zane's tyrannical rule.

Lofty plans, she chastised herself when she still hadn't

managed to free herself from the tower and castle grounds, though the gods knew she'd tried. She'd never been allowed to leave the perfectly smooth, conical stone structure once she'd been imprisoned here. She didn't know enough about the island and its secrets, though she'd heard the guards mention the wild animals roaming freely about the forests, and the quicksand and treacherous swamps she might have to navigate if she ever freed herself from the tower. But with her brother on his way, she wanted to try and reach him halfway.

Another key was inserted in the lock to her door, and she wondered why her ward just didn't separate the key to this room from all the rest so she wouldn't have to try all the keys out every time.

None of the guards or servants she managed to speak to would tell her about King Inari who owned the castle except that he excelled at battle, and he called her his niece, which didn't bode well since, as far as she knew, she had no other living relations. If anyone knew anything more than that, they would not say.

She lifted her black velvet gown and climbed onto the pillow-covered window seat. Leaning out the window, she attempted to guess the distance to the next window, around ten feet down. If she could reach it, maybe she could make it to the bottom floor without getting caught this time.

Several keys had grated in the lock of her door, and finally one made the clicking sound that meant the key holder had finally found the right one. Mirabella jumped off the seat and wheeled around, her heart thundering. She knew no one would suspect she'd make another escape attempt, not now that two stout male guards accompanied the servants when they brought her food or bathwater. Not after the last time that she managed to overpower the woman who was in charge of her, the scrawny-faced Ephyra, serving as her lady-in-waiting. Her heart sped up with concern just the same.

The heavy oak door swung open, and Ephyra walked in, a tray in her hands. Her icy blue eyes took in Mirabella's appearance as she always did, ensuring that Mirabella was still alive and well.

Mirabella straightened her gown and she put on her usual annoyed expression because the woman always looked so annoyed at her, as if she couldn't stand working for her. Well, Mirabella would be happy to leave of her own accord and the woman wouldn't have to do anything!

"Your face is flushed. You're not feverish are you?" Ephyra dropped the tray on the table where two chairs sat, one for Mirabella and one for Ephyra, but she didn't wait for a response, as if she really didn't care. "Eat up and be quick about it. Your betrothed comes to...inspect you."

"Betrothed," Mirabella said, her skin instantly chilled. She stiffened her back and hardened her eyes. "Did my brother sell me to some man?" She walked over to the table for two and lifted a piece of bread from the tray.

She'd even stopped eating for a time, but she would have only weakened herself when she needed to toughen herself instead.

Ephyra's thin lips curved upward, but no warmth reached her eyes. "Lord Leogane Wendover doesn't want *you*; seems there's someone else he prefers to wed. Imagine that?" The woman swiped a blueberry tart from the tray and lifted it to her lips with her little finger elevated as if she were seated at a royal dinner.

No need for pretense here.

Mirabella dropped onto a velvet-covered chair and poked a spoon into a boar-and-brasey broth. "What does my brother say about this?"

"He has nothing to say about it. King Inari is sending the duke here to inspect you. That's what." Ephyra motioned to a girl about Mirabella's age, standing near the doorway. "Justina, bring Princess Mirabella's new gown, and be quick about it."

Mirabella didn't recognize the girl, but then that wasn't so unusual. King Inari often switched out the staff to ensure that none of them grew fond of her. Ephyra was the exception.

The guards and servants were careful not to get close to her, fearing reprisals from the king. If not that, Mirabella had accomplished several escapes over the last few months, though she hadn't managed to get very far. Many of the staff, if not all, were wary of her motives.

Then hope flickered. Mirabella almost allowed herself a smile but quashed the notion when she saw Ephyra watching her. Surely, Leogane would give her some freedom, if her brother didn't reach her in time. If so, she would escape the duke. She would not be the wife to anyone who pledged his allegiance to Inari.

"What are you thinking, princess?" Ephyra asked, her eyes narrowed. "You have a way of looking past a body when you are planning something. Your jaw tightens and..." She glanced down at Mirabella's hands. "You clench your fists."

Mirabella unclenched her hands, made an effort to relax her expression, and grabbed her spoon again. The boar, onions, and potatoes that swam in the thick creamy broth tasted especially good this afternoon. She wondered if Ephyra sampled a good enough quantity before every meal, though she looked like she ate nothing more than a pigeon's egg daily. "I was thinking how much I would not like to see this man, who does not wish me for a bride." She was thinking she would pretend she would go along with the plan. If he could come to take her away from here, mayhap he would get her close enough to where her brother was, and she could leave the island with Argon instead.

"Tsk, tsk, my lady. 'Tis not your choice, but his. Moreover, if you have any idea of making him dislike you anymore than he already does, think again. King Inari has another nobleman in mind for you, and I am certain he would be even more to your disliking. Though rumors abound he wishes your hand and is angered the king has chosen Leogane over him. Nevertheless, Leogane has been loyal to Inari for some years, whereas, Vladek has only just begun to take an interest in Nocices."

But Mirabella wouldn't be anyone's wife that King Inari decided! She was getting out of the tower though and somehow, she had to make contact with Argon so he could take her to real freedom.

"SOMEONE ELSE IS COMING for your sister," Talamaya warned Argon, having seen another one of her visions.

Argon glanced at the princess, everyone moving through the woods with their eyes peeled for any signs of trouble. "Who?"

"A suitor. A duke. He is Leogane of Wendover. I've never heard of him."

"Neither have I. You see this?"

"Aye. In my mind's eye. And he's not happy about the prospect."

"Nobody can wed my sister without my approval," Argon said, furious beyond measure.

Kersta glanced at Argon. "Or your sister's approval, aye?"

"It seems she has no say in it, but there is another who wishes her instead," Talamaya said. "And he is more dangerous than the first."

"They came to the island, or they live here?" Argon wondered if the island was big enough to accommodate three kingdoms. He didn't answer Kersta's question, though he intended it to be his sister's choice if he thought her suitor was good enough for Mirabella.

"They came here. Or at least I see King Leogane's ship flying flags emblazoned with golden lions, off the"—Talamaya frowned—"uh, opposite coast where we landed. So he will be taking her away from the castle while we are trying to reach it in the center of the island."

"He will face the same perils as us then." Which didn't bode well. Argon didn't want his sister hurt at any cost. But if he lost her to this man and his ship, then they'd have to chase Leogane's ship down and battle it out to have his sister returned.

How could this nightmare get any worse than this?

"It can, believe me. You would know that if you had journeyed with us before," Kersta said.

Argon frowned at her. Kersta had read his mind!

"Aye, I have. And I'm glad you would give your sister a choice of who she might have for a husband." Kersta gave him a vague smile.

"How is the one suitor dangerous?" Gallant asked.

"Leogane is a great warrior and undefeated in battle," Talamaya said. "His name means lion."

"And the other?" Gallant turned his head to peer into the dark woods further.

"His men fall easily if killed in the right manner, but he has many more of them."

Gallant looked puzzled.

"They must be beheaded or stabbed in the heart. Any place else and they will not die," Talamaya said.

"See? That is what we need to know first, woman. Not last." Gallant shook his head.

"They can control minds if they catch your gaze," Talamaya further warned.

"That is also good to know." A twig snapped and Gallant swung around, readying his hammer.

AT THE CASTLE, Ephyra acted as though Mirabella had said nothing. She rattled on. "Still, if Leogane doesn't wish you, the king intends to offer you to Vladek. He has already said he wants you, sight unseen." She raised a dark brow. "Though I think the king is a bit suspicious of why this Vladek suddenly is interested in King Inari's niece. But the notion of tying another region under his jurisdiction that he has no control over now appeals." Ephyra snatched the last of the blueberry tarts. "Quit dawdling with your food."

The girl with Mirabella's new gown cleared her throat as she reentered the chamber.

Ephyra motioned for the maid to bring her the light blue velvet gown. "If you are eating no more than that, it is time to dress, *princess*."

She was the only one Mirabella knew who could make the title of princess sound like a disease. Mirabella stared at the fabric with annoyance. "You know I only wear black."

"You have been in mourning for your father for months. 'Tis long enough. And the black does nothing for your pale complexion."

A bell clanged in the inner courtyard and Mirabella's heart jumped. It only sounded when the king arrived, though there had been no mention he was coming, so she assumed it was for Leogane.

"God's teeth," Ephyra said, her face red. "What is he doing here so soon? Stand outside the door," she ordered the guards. "Time to change your gown, princess."

Mirabella stood, hating that her legs felt like soggy noodles.

She'd never feared anyone before Zane turned into Argon's evil twin.

Though Ephyra expected Mirabella to stand up and have her gown changed, instead, she headed for the window, knocking over a vase holding a single blood rose in her haste, and rescued it off the floor. Then peering out of the window, she endeavored to see what the man looked like. Thirty or so men rode into the inner bailey, stirring up dirt, scattering chickens that squawked and sent a flurry of feathers flying, like a sudden snowstorm.

All of the men wore armor to protect themselves from wild animals and other beasties on the island and anything else that preyed on the weak. All were helmed, and all looked the same from her prison forty feet above the ground.

One looked up to see her peeking out the narrow window while she breathed in the rose's sweet fragrance, then as if given an order to look too, everyone shifted their gazes upward, following the first man's gaze.

Her whole body heated, though she did not duck away from the window, just glowered at them. She was certain they could not see the look of contempt on her face from this distance. When they began to dismount, their attention turned to the servants who took their horses. Ephyra roughly tugged her away from the window. "Unless you wish the duke to see you naked first, you best come away from there while you dress."

Mirabella scoffed under her breath and set the rose in a tankard of water.

Within minutes, Mirabella was wearing the soft blue dress and thought how hard it would be to blend in with the woods, though she was not altogether happy about wearing anything other than black. Not until her brother hanged for murdering her father. Then she would wear any color she chose. But this wouldn't work for the woods, she thought. Then again, she really needed to wear trews and a shirt, not a long gown that would catch on the underbrush and tree branches when she made her escape.

After braiding her hair with pearls, Ephyra looked her over and nodded. "That will do."

A knock ensued and when Justina answered the door, the guard said to Ephyra, "His Grace, Duke Leogane wishes to see Princess Mirabella at once. He has other pressing business and doesn't wish to be held up."

"I thought he would stay the evening," Ephyra said. "I thought he would sup with her tomorrow before he left. How will he decide if he wants her if he doesn't spend any time with her?" She spoke in an annoyed way, not truly asking the question of anyone. "Very well, princess, come, and be quick..."

"About it," Mirabella said, wondering if the woman could ever think of something different to say.

Ephyra narrowed her eyes at her. She wasn't allowed to beat Mirabella, but the woman gave her looks that could kill in lieu of the beatings. A time or two Mirabella was sure Ephyra added something to her food that made her sicker than a worm-ridden dog.

Through the cold hall to the circular stone steps and all the way down to the bottom floor, Mirabella reminded herself that she would most likely be able to escape Leogane should he want her, though she couldn't help the way her legs shook or the way her stomach wouldn't quit flip-flopping all over the place.

Between being annoyed the duke would look her over like she was a side of beef, and the fact that no male ever paid her any mind all the time she'd been held prisoner, she couldn't help the way her body reacted to her fear. Luckily, the long sleeves that draped down to the hem of her skirt at the back of her wrists covered the chill bumps dotting her arms. But she was sure her face would reveal much more than she wished to.

Either she'd lose all her color if the man was a beast, or her cheeks would flame rose red if he looked at her in an interested way.

The ten men sat at the elevated table, as if they were the duke and his senior advisors. Servants had hastily prepared a meal for the duke and his men of the same foods she had been offered. Her chin held high, she walked toward the table, bypassing the rest of the empty trestles, two stout fierce-looking guards at her side. All they needed were barbed collars and drooling jowls to make the picture more complete. King Inari had removed any guard who'd seemed in the least bit sympathetic to her cause, and since then had found the nastiest, ugliest beasts to guard her.

Ephyra and Justina hung back at the entrance to the great hall, waiting to hear what was said. Feeling she was going forward to her execution, Mirabella imagined the executioner moving her hair to the top of her head, readying her neck for his blade. The hair on the nape of her neck stood on end.

The man sitting at the center of the table—his shoulder-length hair black as a bottomless well, his eyes ice blue, but clearer than Ephyra's, his lips set in a thin grim line—watched her approach like a hawk targeting a rabbit for its next meal. A scar cut across his cheek, leaving an angry white welt raised against bronzed skin. His dark brows narrowed at the sight of her, and she wasn't sure then, if she'd be able to escape this man's cage any more than she could escape King Inari's tower.

"I have been told you do not wish me." Mirabella tilted her chin up even further.

Ephyra gasped. The duke said nothing, but stared at her, seemingly surprised she would speak, and probably more than surprised at the words she conveyed.

She continued. "Therefore, I offer myself to Count Vladek." Mirabella curtseyed in the courtliest manner, turned, and headed back to the isolation of her chambers which she hoped would give her brother time to reach the castle and take her away from here. Not that she was truly offering herself to Count Vladek, whoever he was. She had thought if Leogane took her from the castle, her brother could meet up with him and then he would free her. But what if her brother was coming from the opposite direction? She'd seen her brother's ship, but not Leogane's. If it was near Argon's, why would she not have seen it?

If Vladek wasn't already here, then her brother would have a chance to come for her instead and steal her away before Vladek arrived. She smiled, her stomach in turmoil, her legs shaky, but her feet already having covered a goodly distance to the exit of the great hall.

"Hold!" the duke boomed.

At least she assumed it was the duke, the way he yelled at her, the sound reverberating off the stone walls of the large room. She paused, as if she'd turned to stone, expecting a beating. But she kept her back to him and wouldn't acknowledge him in anyway, other than not moving forward to the shelter of her chamber, like she wanted to do with all her heart.

"Bring her here!"

Mirabella suspected he was furious with her for not turning to face him. It was rude to ignore her potential husband in that way. But she hoped he wouldn't want her, if he had any notion of the kind, and she would leave with her brother instead.

At once, the guards seized her arms and turned her around, then marched her straight back to the head table. Though she tried to keep up appearances, she felt as though a sudden blizzard had encased her whole body in a block of ice and she imagined her face was as colorless.

Leogane glowered at her, his gaze focused on her eyes, as if he were showing her who commanded her now, his face ablaze and his jaw ticking with anger.

She tried to wriggle free, but the guards only gripped her tighter.

Lifting his tankard, the duke took a swig of his wine, then slammed the copper tankard down with a bang.

Did he think to intimidate her? Only her evil brother did. And only because he murdered or beat those who didn't agree with him once he'd taken over the princedom. She didn't believe the duke would truly beat or kill her, though the angry look on his face indicated he wished to.

"You will not make my decision for me. You—"

"I understand you don't want me. Count Vladek—"

"Cease your prattle, woman!"

She raised her brows in surprise. She was a princess! She gritted her teeth and narrowed her eyes. If he took her as his wife, she would make every effort to escape her new imprisonment if Argon failed to come for her before she left the island.

4

Not expecting King Inari to suddenly offer his only niece to Leogane in marriage, all his own plans had been scattered to the wind. They'd had their difficulties between the kingdoms, and they needed peace for both their kingdoms to prosper. Before that, Leogane had every intention of marrying his chief advisor's daughter, the dark-haired beauty, Leetonia, sweet and civil-tongued, opposite of everything Princess Mirabella seemed to be. Hot headed, ill mannered, spoiled rotten, and used to getting her way, he imagined. He hadn't even known King Inari had a niece, so that had been a real surprise.

Even now, he could see she thought she was the one making the decisions around here. He shook his head and leaned back on the fur-covered chair.

Her golden hair was neatly braided in two long ropes extending to her knees and decorated in shimmering pearls. The soft blue gown swept over her slight figure, but her liquid brown eyes turned nearly black and her full pink lips scowling back at him made him believe she would make the worst sort of bride. She seemed to despise him as much as he loathed marrying her just to produce an heir...

He shook his head at the ludicrous thought. He'd had every intention of looking her over and rejecting her. That was his plan until the viper told him she'd offer herself to Count Vladek. No one knew anything of the man, except that he was uncommonly handsome, dark-haired and eyed, and had a mesmerizing quality about him. Even King Inari seemed to be drawn under Vladek's spell, when here he, Leogane, had fostered the best of relations with the king for the most part and might lose that edge if the king gave his niece to Vladek.

Besides, a smoldering inferno still raged deep inside him, as he believed the attacks on him and his men, three times on their way to Castle Mayen, were more than mere coincidence. Some of Count Vladek's men? Sent to discourage him in his task?

His jaw set, Leogane deepened his voice and firmly said, "You will return with me to Castle Grance."

Her mouth dropped open and her eyes widened.

He smiled, enjoying for the moment that he'd jousted with Princess Mirabella and won. Turning to Ephyra he said, "Have the lady dressed and ready for the long journey ahead. You may send the young girl standing beside you to accompany her."

"What about me?" Ephyra asked, her voice trembling.

"What about you?" he asked, annoyed. The woman looked like she would die on the journey she was so thin, and he wouldn't want to risk it. Besides, once he returned home, he would select maids on his own staff to take care of the princess, not someone of Inari's choice. Even the woman who accompanied her now would be sent home after they arrived safely at the castle.

Ephyra straightened her shoulders and tried to make herself appear more determined or perhaps more in charge of the situation. "I have been given the mission to watch over Princess Mirabella until she's wed, by order of the king himself."

Leogane narrowed his eyes and leaned forward. "Do as I say now," he growled. He was not used to underlings telling him they wouldn't do as he commanded.

"At once, my lord." Ephyra quickly curtsied, then motioned to the guards. "Hurry, bring her with us and be quick about it!"

For now, he didn't intend to wed the woman. Instead, he would observe her actions for the next couple of weeks. If she was a holy terror as he suspected, Count Vladek could have her with Leogane's blessing. If she wasn't...

Leogane didn't even want to go down that dark alley.

IN THE WOODS, a little brown rabbit scampered through the underbrush and that's what Gallant had heard and seen. He took a relieved breath and they all continued to walk through the forest at a quickened pace.

"We will save her," Kersta reassured Argon. She thought the world of him for caring so much about his sister and wanting to keep her safe. "She can come to any of our kingdoms for safekeeping until you are able to take over your princedom and put the situation aright."

"And we are paid the mountain of gold you have offered for this deed." Gallant narrowed his eyes at Argon. "Ye dinna have the gold, do ye? Your brother has it."

"But it is mine by right and you will get your payment sooner or later," Argon said.

Gallant snorted.

"And thank you, Kersta, for the offer. I may have to take you up on it. I won't be able to take Mirabella home with me until 'tis safe," Argon said.

"You're welcome, and Kersta is right," Talamaya said.

Kersta noticed Mexia was quiet. "Is something the matter?" she whispered to Mexia.

"I sense we are not alone," Mexia said.

"I could have told you that," Gallant grumbled.

They heard what sounded like horses approaching them through the forest, but they couldn't see them for the dense fog that suddenly began to fill the woods like a dark omen.

"Steady," Gallant told his weapon.

Kersta and the other ladies readied their staffs. Argon had his sword at the ready.

To Kersta's surprise, two centaurs came out of the misty woods—a male and a female with chestnut appaloosa bodies and chests and faces of humans, wearing bows and quivers of arrows. The woman wore a leather tunic trimmed in beads; the male wore only leather bracers on his bronzed arms. Both were dark haired, their hair tied back in tails. Unless things were different on this island, Kersta had found it was easy to befriend them.

"We are friend not foe," Argon quickly said. "My sister has been imprisoned in the tower on this island and I'm here to free her."

"Her uncle imprisoned her?" the male centaur asked, sounding surprised.

"My uncle has been dead for many years. My twin brother sold her to a man who must now be claiming he is her uncle and wishes to have her married off to a man I know nothing of."

"This island is dangerous for any who venture here," the centaur said, the female remaining quiet.

"But you live here," Talamaya said.

The male inclined his head. "We were born here. We fight any manner of man or beast that doesn't allow us to live here in peace."

"Just the two of you?" Argon asked. "If you would like to leave here and join more of your kind, we can take you with us."

"We know of a whole group of centaurs who live in an area where it's peaceful," Kersta said.

"What do you plan to do?" the male asked.

"Rescue my sister and take her to one of the ladies' king-doms until I can take over my own princedom from my brother who vanquished Mirabella here," Argon said.

"There are many of my kind here, thanks for offering us a new home. But this is our home. We have word other men have gone to the castle, and now others have come for the woman—your sister," the man said. "We will take you on the best path that leads to the castle."

"But we believe Leogane is taking my sister to his ship on the opposite side of the island," Argon said. "Would it not be quicker to stop him before he reaches the shore instead of heading for the castle?"

"You would not survive if you head in any other direction. Have you seen the kishi?" the male centaur asked.

"Aye," Argon said.

"There are more than fifty on this island. Also goblins will steal your food and cheetaurs will rob you of your life," the centaur said.

Kersta sighed. "Oh, cheetaurs, we've had our dealings with them in the past."

"We'll lead the way." The centaurs began to walk through the woods ahead of them.

Argon hoped they weren't being led astray.

"We aren't," Kersta said, taking Argon's arm and leaning close to him to whisper the words so the centaurs couldn't hear her, though Argon hadn't spoken his thoughts aloud, so they wouldn't know what Kersta was remarking about. "Goblins! At least ten of them!"

They might be small, hairy little beasts, but they were quick, helmed, wearing capes and partial armor. They played tricks on humans, stole their food, and tried to scare them off.

"The food! They're after our food!" Gallant said, swinging his hammer at them, keeping them away from his food pack.

Kersta tossed her food pack into the woods and the goblins headed for the bread and smoked fish while the companions hurried on their way. She noticed the centaurs were watching the way the companions handled the situation. If they had battled the goblins, she figured the centaurs wouldn't have helped them any further.

Gallant grouched. "Woman, you threw away good food for naught. Dinna think I'll share mine with you now."

Argon smiled at Kersta. "I'll share mine with you, Kersta. Thanks for dealing successfully with the trouble."

"Sometimes the simplest gesture can resolve issues instead of having to deal with it in a battle to the death," Kersta said.

"Wait until they finish the food and come back for the rest of our food packs," Gallant said.

Kersta swore she heard the female centaur give a small laugh. But that wasn't their next real problem. They were approaching huge boulders that reminded her of deserts and boulders and cheetaurs.

"The cheetaurs live here," the male centaur said. "Keep an eye out."

The cheetaurs were extremely speedy predators, great jumpers, and their sharp, long teeth were lethal. Suddenly they appeared in a pack of six on top of one of the largest boulders. They counted the companions' numbers and Kersta knew they were ready for a fight. They were beautiful creatures but deadly adversaries.

"Use our staffs on stun, right?" Kersta asked, taking a stance to fight them.

"Aye, if we can knock them out, do it," Talamaya said.

Kersta noticed the centaurs had their bows readied, but they weren't taking any of the cheetaurs out before the big cats lunged.

Then the cats jumped, each of them going for the humans on foot and one small, bearded dwarf.

The ladies all managed to knock out a cheetaur with their magically enhanced staffs. The remaining three cheetaurs hesitated and then turned and jumped back on top of the boulders. The cheetaurs might have wanted to fight them, to kill them, but the cheetaurs recognized when they were beat.

Kersta was glad Argon and Gallant had held back and hadn't killed the other cheetaurs. It appeared the centaurs approved also, but as they began their journey again, both Argon and Kersta walked so they could watch behind them. Cheetaurs were known to attack when they saw movement. If Argon and Kersta turned their backs on the big cats, that could be dangerous. But the cheetaurs were checking out their fallen brethren instead. And then in a protective mode, the cheetaurs stayed with their sleeping family.

"Any other surprises?" Mexia asked the centaurs.

"You may have trouble with Leogane if he decides he wants to keep Mirabella," the female centaur said. "Maybe you can work out an arrangement with him once you take over your princedom. Maybe your sister is interested in him even."

Argon took a deep breath. "I will keep an open mind."

But Kersta thought he didn't like the idea that someone would offer for his sister whom he didn't know. She didn't blame him either.

"The others—led by a Count Vladek? They are treacherous," the female centaur said. "With Leogane, he will listen to what you have to say. Count Vladek's men? Not a chance. If your staffs can be set to something more lethal when you encounter them, be sure to use them that way. We have had to kill a dozen of them already. We've never encountered beings like them before here on the island. They are after the princess. They can mesmerize the unsuspecting before ripping their throats out. Aim for their hearts with your blades and hammer. Removing their heads will stop them also. If you only stun them, they will be back for your blood."

"Aye, we will," Talamaya said. "We will."

5

Within the hour, Leogane and his party had departed Castle Mayen, thirty of his best trained knights dressed in chain mail and ready for any battle, Princess Mirabella and her maid, Justina, the girl not much older than the princess, about her height, but golden-haired and quiet. Leogane couldn't help wondering if he'd lost his mind. He noticed Justina seemed much relieved to leave Castle Mayen behind, unlike the princess who appeared to be nervous about her surroundings.

Leogane glanced over his shoulder to see the princess and her maid riding behind him in silence. Mirabella just watched the woods, as men rode on either side of the ladies, and others followed behind. Three more scouted up ahead, while two rode in front of Leogane, ever vigilant in watching for an ambush. He had no doubt whoever had sent men to attack him before, would do so again, but he was certain, they would be careful not to injure the princess.

Justina's gaze caught his, then she looked over at her mistress, and back to Leogane. He wondered then, how long the girl had served the princess. What secrets could she tell him?

Once they stopped for the night, he would question her thoroughly. In the meantime, he would question Mirabella. "Ride up with me, princess!" Leogane commanded.

She kicked her horse to a canter and joined him, refusing to look his way.

Her action both amused and annoyed him. He studied the tilt of her proud chin and of her royal bearing, wondering for the first time why she'd been secreted away to the isolated Castle Mayen. Except for a small guard force, and a smaller number of servants, the naturally well-fortified castle and grounds were not used for anything else that he could see, but to house one ill-tempered princess. Nobody seemed to like her, which was evident in the way her guards handled her, and even the woman in charge of her seemed to despise the princess, only wishing to maintain her position as her guardian a while longer for appearance's sake, no doubt. Which confirmed Mirabella was a terror.

Why hide her away? Was it to keep her out of the clutches of greedy men, none of whom the king wanted her to wed? With her contemptible disposition, she would find no husband who would give her room to act poorly toward the staff, if the man had any backbone at all. Certainly, *he* wouldn't permit her to give his staff any grief and would lock her in a tower if she said one unkind word to the lowest of his servants.

"Why were you living at Mayen Castle?" he asked, stifling the correct protocol to call her princess. Her kind hadn't earned the privilege of their class. As a knight, he'd learned to be chivalrous and kind to those who were in need. He couldn't quash the contempt he felt for her, and every other woman or man like her who used their title and privilege to their advantage, hurting those who served them in the process.

She didn't answer him.

Unused to insubordination, he was having a devil of a time remembering he was a knight as well as a duke, and that he needed to keep his temper in check. Despite this, he growled, "Answer me now!"

She tilted her chin up higher and pursed her lips.

Grabbing her reins, he pulled her horse to a stop. "Would you prefer walking?" Not that he wanted her to walk. They would never get anywhere, and he imagined she'd blister her feet and be a mess. But maybe walking would knock some of the willfulness out of her.

She glared at him; her brown eyes flickered with a red-hot flame. "You can bully me all you like, Your Grace," she hissed. "But know this, there is only one man I fear, and it is my evil brother. So do your worse, duke." She whipped her head around and stared straight ahead.

For a moment, he glowered at her in stunned silence. He had no idea what to say to her. No one spoke in such a manner to him. Come to think of it, not even his enemies when captured would speak to him thus. The idea grated on him that she was right. There was very little he could do to her to make her talk. But he wondered, as fearless as she appeared, and it didn't seem to be a show, why she would fear her brother and he hadn't heard of him either.

Leogane released her reins and motioned for her to continue walking her horse beside him. "If you think you will anger me enough to give you up to Vladek, think again."

She glanced at him, her look bewildered.

Instantly, he wondered why he'd even said what he did, now having no intention of making the witch his wife.

Once they'd gone a short distance into the Larimar Forest, Mirabella tightened her hands around her reins, making her knuckles turn white. Her face lost all its color, and her brown eyes searched for signs of something.

He hadn't heard or seen anything, nor had his men indicated anything was the matter. "What ails you? Did you hear or see anything amiss?" he asked, wondering if she were afraid of the woods.

"I've...I've never been in the forest before. I...I hear all kinds of strange sounds."

He gave a short bark of laughter to which she responded with a sharp glance of resentment. "Sorry, my lady," he said, mocking the prim, proper princess who'd never ventured out of the castle, too afraid to muddy the hems of her gowns, he suspected. "I hadn't realized you'd never left the grounds of your castle."

"I have never left the tower," she replied curtly, her dark brows furrowed, her mouth pinched in annoyance.

He laughed again. "Worse even still." Then he studied her, though she quickly turned her face away. "You are not one of those souls who are afraid to venture beyond your chamber, are you?" He'd heard of creatures like that, who were so morti-fied of what lay beyond their room, they lived and died there, never having ventured forth their entire lives. He could not have a wife like that, who would need to help run his staff, and keep the castle in good order when he and his men went to battle.

"Why would you desire to wed me when you know so little about me?" she asked.

"I do *not* desire to wed you."

The scowl returned to her face, and she looked away, but her question made him think she had not had a choice about staying in her chamber. Had her uncle worried men would gain access to her, if she weren't well hidden away? On the other hand, was it that she'd tried to escape her uncle's rule?

Now that created new lumps in his porridge. If the lady was that willful...

Again, he shook his head, wondering how he'd gotten himself into this mess. "Why, pray tell, did you stay in your chamber?" He might as well ask, though he was not sure he would hear the truth when she gave him her version.

At first, she didn't answer, and he knew she was testing his resolve once again, but then she turned her ear toward the north, and he thought he heard something too. Something ominous. Like before when he and his men had been attacked.

A flock of birds flew into the trees from the same direction, and Leogane shouted, "Form a circle around the women!" His heart thundered against his ribs as he pulled his sword from its scabbard. He was not afraid for himself or his men, but he worried about having the women in their midst. It could make fighting more difficult.

"What is it?" Mirabella asked.

"We were attacked by men three times on the journey here. I believe they were some of Count Vladek's men."

"How could you say such a thing? Accuse an innocent man of wrongdoing just—"

"Silence, woman!"

Blinking her eyes, she stared at him.

"They wore a crest on the tunics covering their chain mail. 'Twas the same as what my people said Vladek wore when he visited the king."

She licked her lips and swallowed hard.

He wasn't sure she believed him, and truly, he shouldn't have cared. It bothered him just the same that she would defend this Count Vladek whom she didn't know, according to her uncle. Unless...

Unless the villain had sneaked into the castle to see her already.

He couldn't think of that now, as his men circled around them. He stayed close to the women, watching for any signs of an ambush.

For what seemed like an eternity, no one moved. The

princess's horse nickered softly, one of his men's horses snorted and pawed the ground uneasily, but it was Mirabella's expression that revealed the first of the onslaught. Her eyes grew big, her lips quavered, and she opened her mouth to cry out well before the enemy was even in sight. He didn't have any time to dwell on her strange actions as fifty or sixty men charged them, wearing black tunics emblazoned with a blood red rose.

As before, the men were good, but not strong enough for his men. It was like they were unused to battling on horseback, unlike his men who jousted when not in battle, and fought on their horses unless they were unseated. They'd grown up in the saddle, and every one of them fought as valiantly as before, delving blow after blow, swords clanking, horses prancing, and charging, circling and backing up, his men decimating the enemies' larger force.

Their enemies' faces were shielded by helms, and again, Leogane wondered if any of these men were Vladek, though he assumed the count waited in hiding, waited for his men to deliver the princess to him, instead, the coward that he was.

Leogane held his position in the inner circle, wanting to help his fellow knights fight the enemy, but forcing himself to remain beside the women in case any of the enemy broke through the outer circle.

The only method that seemed to kill the enemy was lopping off their heads; cuts to the arms or legs didn't slow them down much and attempting to penetrate their chain mail to reach their hearts was nigh to impossible. Yet, one of his greatest archers had taken a lance and speared one of the enemies in the heart during an earlier battle and successfully killed the brigand. And another archer had managed to pierce the mail with a crossbolt.

When the last of the men lay dead, and his own men raised

their swords in triumph, Leogane looked over at Mirabella and saw her face as gray as granite.

"They're not real," she said, her voice hushed.

"They're very real," Leogane assured her, and motioned for one of his knights to remove the helm from a decapitated head.

When the knight lifted the helm off the ground, a pile of dust poured out.

"What the..." Leogane stared at the empty helm. "Check the rest."

Not only had the heads disappeared, the bodies themselves had disintegrated into dust.

"Magic users," one of the men said, cursing. His green eyes hot with hatred, he turned to Leogane. "Black magic."

"They're not dead," Mirabella whispered, tears clogging her throat.

"They're dead," Leogane reassured her, hoping to stay his men's concerns as well. He didn't need panic on his hands. They'd never bothered to check the other men they'd killed before, leaving them for their lord to recover and bury, not wishing to delay their journey in the inhospitable woods. They were also on the lookout for more of the kishi, like the human-hyena faced ones that had dropped onto their ship and died upon impact. A third one was dropped out to sea, and he wondered what magic users on the island had killed their enemy in such a way. They'd never employed a mage and he was afraid of coming up against one so powerful.

"The men we just killed are dead," Leogane said again, and motioned for his men to move out. "Are you going to be all right, Princess?"

She nodded, but she didn't look well.

"A cottage is located a couple of miles ahead. A healer's hut. We'll stop there and you ladies can rest." Though he wished it not, as the stop would delay their journey overmuch. It had

taken them a day and a half to reach the castle in the beginning. They should have dropped anchor on the other side of
the island. Mayhap it would have taken less time. On the return
trip to his ship, he had hoped to make better time, but they
were fighting the same entities as before and they had two
women to think of also. Now he assumed it would take much
more time.

"Thank you." The fight was no longer in Mirabella's words,
and he wondered if the lady truly was a recluse and the journey
and fighting were too much for her. He'd never considered she
might die on the journey because she was too frail to manage.

"Have you ever met this Count Vladek?" he asked, hoping to
get her mind off the battle, if that's what still distressed her.

She stared at him with the oddest look, as if she didn't quite
know the answer to his question. Was she in shock?

"Princess Mirabella, have you ever personally met the man
at Castle Mayen?"

She shook her head and pulled her gaze away from his.

However, there was something she wasn't telling him, something that bothered her, and subsequently bothered him more
than anything. What was she hiding?

'TWAS TRUE MIRABELLA had never been in the woods before that
she could recall, having been drugged and once she was incarcerated in the tower, she'd managed to escape, but only to be
caught on the first floor of the castle, and 'twas true she wasn't
used to all the strange sounds of the forest here, but there was
something more to Mirabella's distress than that. She'd heard
whispered words when no one else had seemed to hear them.
She heard the men scouting up ahead speaking to each other
from time to time, joking with each other about her unsuit-

ability to marry their lord, betting whether he would wed her or his advisor's daughter.

Her skin chilled with the notion. For too many months she'd lived in veritable isolation but being with people now did not improve her life. She'd wanted to escape her captivity, but most of all, she wanted to right a wrong, to punish her brother for murdering her father and stealing the crown, to help ensure Argon ruled the princedom himself, not like the tyrant Zane was, but as a good ruler like her father had been.

She hadn't wanted the aggressors to slay her escort, yet she had not wanted the "enemy" killed either. She'd sworn that the count had whispered her name, saying he wanted her, desired to bring her home to her mother's people. She'd never known who her mother's people had been in truth, her mother dying when she was born.

Glancing at Leogane, she found him watching her. He seemed concerned for her welfare, which dissolved some of her animosity for him.

The savage fighting hadn't bothered her as much as the whispered words that had filled her head, or the strange fact that her hearing seemed to be growing more sensitive by the day. It made her think she was losing her mind.

Closing her eyes, she listened to an animal lapping at a stream nearby and heard a bird of prey whoosh down to the forest floor, snatching a squeaking mouse in its wicked talons. When she opened her eyes, she expected to see the animal and the bird, but neither were anywhere in sight. She had never had this acute sense of hearing before either, not until a few nights ago.

At first, she had ignored it, or tried to.

But standing at her window back at Mayen Castle, she'd even begun to hear the soldiers complain about how boring their job was while they surveyed the surrounding land from the wall walk encircling the inner bailey. Even on still days when there was no breeze to carry their voices. Even on windy days when the air circulated well away from the castle. Was it a magic user's gift? Was it because she was nearly seventeen?

She heard no more whispers in the woods, other than the low talking of some of their escort, some fearing the enemy were magic users. A ripple of chills cascaded down her arms and she pulled her black cloak tighter.

At least she'd ridden a horse since she was a wee thing so she was comfortable with riding for days. The roan horse seemed to take to her at once and she was glad to befriend her. She wondered if she might be able to win Justina over now that the girl was no longer under Ephyra's or the guards' influence. She needed an ally, no matter who the person was.

Once they stopped at the healer's hut—as it seemed the duke intended for Mirabella to ride at his side until that time—she would speak to the girl and find out all she could about King Inari's court and attempt to make friends with her.

She glanced at the duke, and despite the scar that ran across his cheek, found him to be a handsome man, though he was too irritating to be her husband. Not only that, she would never agree to be any man's wife who was devoted to serving a man who claimed to be her uncle. The duke turned to look at her, and she quickly looked away, her cheeks heating.

He chuckled under his breath. "It seems your cheeks are no longer a sickly gray, but have a rosy color to them now, my lady."

"'Tis the chill in the air, duke." Even though the air was perfectly warm.

"Ah. You have not told me why you remained in your chamber."

Glaring at him, she said, "You are the king's loyal vassal. You serve him whether he has done wrong or not. Would it matter to you that my evil brother sold me to the man called Inari? That this king you speak of is *not* my uncle? That my brother Zane murdered my father?"

Leogane stared at her in surprise, but for several minutes didn't respond. Was it because he was a titled lord, and careful to choose the proper words in response? Either that or he thought her a liar. Then her heart sank. Surely, the king would say she would lie about all this as soon as Leogane removed her from the castle. Inari couldn't afford to have a vassal lord suddenly turn on him to seek vengeance because he was trying to pawn off a niece who was not his niece on Leogane.

"It doesn't matter what I say, because you will not believe me."

For a moment, Leogane didn't reply. Then finally, he nodded and looked away. She'd had a passing hope that mayhap Leogane would take her side in this, but she knew only Argon could bring justice to their princedom and make their brother pay.

She longed for someone to care about her, to avenge her father's death, but Leogane would never be that man.

I care, the wind whispered, the sound darkly seductive, strangely close, yet far away. She whipped her head around and saw nothing. She knew then she was losing her mind.

6

K ersta and her party were still following the centaurs when the black cloaked and armored knights rushed them in the forest from all directions.

"Attack!" the male centaur said, and Kersta knew these were the knights they'd warned them about.

"Don't look into their eyes!" the female centaur shouted, reminding them of the danger.

But Kersta was too busy fighting a knight brandishing his broadsword at her to focus on anything but his weapon. She figured he thought he could cut her staff in half with a heavy swing of his sword, but Modi had made their staffs so strong, no ordinary sword could slice them in two. Instead, the knight's steel met her staff, striking hard, but it bounced off and nearly made him lose hold of his sword. Still, doing her usual staff attacks wouldn't work. They each carried short swords also in case of an emergency, but they wouldn't reach past the knights' broadswords. On the other hand, their staffs had great reach. On another quest, when Kersta had used her staff on a dark elf who had been attempting to kill her, she'd hit him once and killed

him instantly. She'd figured she would have had much more of a
fight since the dark elves were so difficult to take down!

In fighting this knight, Kersta's staff did nothing to stop him.
She blocked his sword thrice and slammed it into his head the
next time. That should have killed him. A blow to the chest
didn't do anything either. Then she remembered what the
centaurs had said—that they needed to be run through the
heart or their head lopped off.

She changed her maneuver and thrust her staff as hard as
she could into the chest of the knight, not believing she could
penetrate his heart through his armor, but it worked! She and
her friends owed Modi their lives countless times over.

The creature screeched, grabbed at his chest, and she
thought she was going to have to fight to pull her staff out of
chest, but she easily pulled her staff out as his body disintegrated and she saw dust on it right as he collapsed—or his
armor collapsed—to the ground. But just as quickly, another
knight took his place.

"Use your staffs like a spear," she hollered to her friends, who
were failing with their usual tactics too. She didn't have time to
see if their new maneuvers aided them then as Gallant swung
his mighty war hammer, decapitating the dark knights as fast as
he could swing his hammer near the princess, protecting her as
always.

Argon stayed between Kersta and Mexia, taking down knight
after knight with a thrust of his sword into their hearts or a
swing at their necks and removing their heads from their bodies
to help them while they learned how to use their staffs effectively against the knights.

A dark knight struck Mexia's staff with his sword with such a
blow, her staff went flying. Argon was about to step in to protect
her when Mexia raised her hands, formed a ball of fire, and

struck the knight in the chest who was attacking her. He laughed in a sinister way.

Argon skewered him with his sword, taking care of the menace, and swung around to take on another knight.

Unlike with the goblins and cheetaurs they had encountered earlier, the centaurs were battling for the lives, targeting knights with their arrows as fast as they could nock the arrows.

Mexia drew her staff to her from where it lay in some bushes further away where the knight had sent it flying. And then with the staff back in her grasp, Mexia shoved it into the heart of another dark knight.

Kersta was still fighting one of her own. The dark knight had seen what the women were doing, and he was effectively blocking her every attempt to skewer him in that manner.

Argon finished another knight off and decapitated the one Kersta was struggling with in a decisive side blow. Hearing no more fighting, Kersta and the others looked around, but to her relief, she didn't see any more of them.

"Thank you." Kersta inclined her head to the prince, knowing he had as much at stake to keep them alive to aid his sister, but she really did like him. A lot.

"Aye, thank you," Mexia said to him also because Argon had stepped in to protect her also.

"We should stay at the castle tonight. It is not very far from here," the male centaur said.

"If Leogane has taken my sister from there already, we must continue after him." Argon didn't want to lose her, Kersta knew.

Kersta agreed, though she'd prefer staying in a castle for the night for safety's sake. That was saying King Inari's guards would even let them in. But she understood Argon's need to catch up to his sister at all costs.

"I will go with you," Kersta said. "If Leogane and his party are fighting these creatures, they are out in the open just like we are. It would be better if we were allies against a common enemy."

"Ye are no' thinking right, woman." Gallant said. "We should stay at the castle for safety sake, rest up, and journey again at first light, ready to fight these dark knights after a good night's sleep. We are apt to perish in the middle of the night if we go traipsing through the woods after dark."

"I will also continue on the quest with you, Argon," Talamaya said. "If we lose your sister, we have lost everything. And I know I would feel the same way as you, if it was my brother who was being held hostage instead."

Gallant grumbled, "You leave me no other choice but to follow you, even if it be the death of me." He turned to speak to the centaurs. "Debt of gratitude," he explained.

Talamaya no longer reminded him his debt of gratitude for saving him had been paid in full several quests ago. They all knew they'd become like family to him no matter how much he groused about things, and he wanted to stay with them.

Kersta wondered what would happen to him when Mexia went off to join her mage husband, and Talamaya joined Lazarion. Kersta was the only one who would actually stay in Damar on the continent of Inherian.

"Mexia?" Talamaya asked.

That was the thing about the princess. She never dictated how things would go. She wanted to know how everyone felt about the quest they would go on.

"Oh, I'm going with you. We have a mission to fulfill and it's not at the castle. The sooner we accomplish it, the sooner Argon takes us home," Mexia said.

They looked to see what the centaurs felt about it.

"This is not our battle. We will direct you on your way, but we'll stay the night at the castle. We wish you the best," the male centaur said.

"Thank you for your help." Argon bowed to them.

They inclined their heads and then the centaurs led the party to the castle and pointed out the direction for them to go to catch up to Leogane. They saw fresh horse droppings left behind like "breadcrumbs" showing them the way.

"Watch where you step," Gallant said, and they all thanked the centaurs and continued on their way.

Kersta had the map out and was reading it, stumbling on rocks and tree roots while trying to see where they were exactly. Argon reached over and took her arm to help her with her footing while she continued to analyze their trek. "You know Leogane and his men and your sister are on horseback and will travel faster than us? I had not considered that."

"I had, but didn't wish to bring it up," Argon admitted. "You and your friends fought well. Your staffs were amazing, but the way you wielded them and were able to adapt your maneuvers to effectively fight the dark knights was extraordinary."

"We've had to adapt our fighting skills as we've journeyed through many dangerous regions. You were amazing too. I've never seen a prince fight with such ferocity and accuracy too while you attempted to protect both Mexia and me until we could begin taking out some of the knights." Kersta and Mexia would never have made it out of that encounter alive if the prince hadn't stepped in to help them.

"And what of me?" Gallant asked, walking in front of Kersta and behind Talamaya and Mexia.

Kersta smiled. "You were Gallant as always."

He scoffed.

The ladies chuckled.

"You were amazing," Talamaya said. "Before Kersta learned how to defeat the dark knights with our staffs, you were cutting down the knights' numbers or we would have perished."

"Aye 'tis true," Gallant said.

Kersta and Argon shared smiles.

Modest Gallant wasn't.

The twilight turned to dark just as they reached the marsh-lands and quicksand featured on the map. Forested wetlands were shadowed in darkness, a full moon's light filtering through some of the tree branches swaying in the breeze making it appear something else was moving in the swamp.

"We have to stop here for the night." Kersta pointed to the area before the swamp. "We can't see by the lantern's light well enough to navigate this treacherous terrain." They could use their fairy light, but it was better used when they had to keep moving because of imminent danger.

"I agree." Talamaya said.

Everyone else agreed except Argon. Kersta knew he wanted to continue on his way no matter the dangers that lay ahead, but he conceded.

ARGON WAS afraid Leogane's party was already at the beach where their ship was moored and first thing in the morning, Leogane would take off on the transports to reach his ship. They would be well out to sea before Argon and the others could ever reach them.

But Kersta and her friends were right in using caution on this part of the island.

He and Kersta gathered firewood while Mexia fetched water to prepare the food.

Gallant watched for danger, his war hammer ready for action. Talamaya was searching through her food pack to make a meal. Argon was impressed at how the ladies, all royalty, had been able to manage on their own like this when women in their part of the world normally would never have left their royal city to go on dangerous quests. Even the gruff dwarf grew on him. He was impressed how the four of them worked together so well as a unified force. He wished his brother had never turned on them like this. Before their father had died, the family had worked together, just like Kersta and her friends.

"I'm sorry about your brother," Kersta said as she and he gathered more firewood, some for the campfire for cooking, some for protecting.

He glanced at Kersta and shook his head. "You read my mind?"

"Aye."

"I will never get used to that."

"It *is* useful."

They brought the twigs and branches back to add to the main campfire where Talamaya was starting a fire with the tinder she'd gathered.

"Did you try to use your ability to clear their minds of thoughts? The dark knights', I mean," Kersta asked Argon as they went back out to gather more firewood for protective fires.

"I was too busy trying to stop them from killing us. I'm sure it wouldn't have done anything to them. If they can control minds, I probably couldn't eliminate their thoughts. Well, hide them. The person could be thinking about something, but I'd just hide the thought from someone like you."

"Like you're doing with me now."

"I cannot help it, now that I'm afraid you'll read my mind."

"Which means you have something to hide? You haven't told me everything about what Modi said to you."

"She speaks in riddles. You know that yourself since you and your companions have spoken to her. Only some of what she said I could understand."

"What about me? That I would find a husband?"

Argon shook his head. "All she said was it would be someone you least expect."

"It better not be Gallant."

"I heard ye, woman," Gallant called out from their campsite. His gruff voice sounded slightly amused.

"I swear he has the best hearing of any of us," Kersta whispered.

"What if the person you are supposed to be with is Leogane? You cannot go with him." Argon didn't want to think of Kersta with either man. Gallant was too disagreeable and Leogane... well, he shouldn't be taking Argon's sister as his wife either.

"Well, maybe it is," she said. "*That* would be unexpected. Why shouldn't I be with him?"

"Neither of them. Because Gallant annoys you all the time and Leogane has taken my sister against her will."

"Hmm, I don't know. But I think there's more to it than that. What will you do if your sister finds favor with Leogane?" Kersta asked.

Argon let out his breath. "In this short amount of time? I doubt it. She has had so many suitors my father wished her to consider, but she wasn't interested in any of them. And after she was taken hostage, and then is being forced to marry this man? I can't imagine she would be interested in marrying him."

"Did Mirabella give a reason about rejecting the other suitors?"

At least Argon was proud of his father for giving Mirabella a say in this, unlike with King Inari. "She said her suitors were too old, mostly. Too young on occasion. One was more interested in how he looked than anything about my sister's appearance. We caught him preening before a mirror on several visits."

Kersta laughed. "You do not preen?"

"Goddess forbid."

They carried the last of the wood back to build the other campfires.

"Do you think there's anything that might crawl out of the swamps at night?" Kersta asked, turning her attention to the area a short distance through the woods.

"I wouldn't know. But we'll need to guard against the dark knights in the woods this eve. Or anything else that might cause us problems," Argon said.

"I can provide a protective barrier shield while we sleep," Mexia said as they all sat down to eat their dried beef, leeks, and potato soup.

"Can you do that and still rest?" Argon asked. Everyone needed plenty of rest to deal with what they might face tomorrow.

"Aye, but I won't be able to use my magic for some time after that. It drains my power," Mexia said.

"Ye could have used it to protect us from the dark knights earlier." Gallant grabbed another piece of dried venison.

"She couldn't. She uses it when we have no other options available," Talamaya said. "Her use of it for tonight is perfect."

Kersta took another bite of her meal, then she asked Argon, "Are you certain you do not have an uncle who could be a king?"

"I didn't believe so, but what if Inari was my mother's brother? I've never known anything about her people."

"Why not?" Mexia pulled apart a piece of brown bread and offered it to Kersta since she'd given hers to the goblins.

"My mother died when my brother and I were two when she gave birth to Mirabella. I don't remember anything about her. We were raised by nannies. Our father had no siblings, no living grandparents, or parents when we were growing up. I never even thought about my mother's family. Probably because no one ever spoke of her or her family."

"That seems odd unless they were estranged. Mayhap your

mother married your father against her own father's wishes. And her family disinherited her, so they had nothing to do with any of her offspring—you and your sister and brother," Talamaya said.

"'Tis possible," Argon agreed.

"So if King Inari is your uncle, your mother's brother, his father and hers had been a king," Talamaya said, then spooned up some more of her soup.

"This is very good," Kersta said.

"Aye, 'tis," Argon and the others agreed. "If my uncle, and my grandfather before him had been king, then my mother would have been a princess from a kingdom instead of from a princedom like I had thought."

"So if your mother was disinherited by your grandfather, why would your uncle now believe he has the right to give Mirabella away to seal a treaty between two territorial rulers? She wouldn't be your uncle's to offer," Talamaya said.

"Which makes me believe my brother Zane gave her to the king for a monetary reward and the king locked her away and then gave her to one of his vassal lords. And I'll put a stop to it."

"What if this king wants to eliminate you because you are attempting to thwart his plan?" Talamaya asked.

"My brother has tried to eliminate me unsuccessfully already." Argon finished his meal. No one was stopping him from rescuing his sister. Though Talamaya had a good point. He already had a battle on one front when he had to fight his brother. He sure didn't need to fight King Inari and Leogane also.

KERSTA WOKE in the middle of the night and realized they were surrounded by dense fog. So dense, she couldn't see anything.

She tried drinking Modi's tea because in similar conditions, it had helped them see through the mist, but not here.

"What's wrong?" Talamaya asked, stirring from sleep.

"The fog is so thick," Kersta whispered. "We cannot see anything in this. Nothing that might be coming after us."

"No wonder it's called the Emerald Isle of Mists," Mexia said. "My protection shield should work. Get some sleep."

But Kersta couldn't sleep with worrying about the fog and what might be in it. She swore she saw something moving in the soupy fog. "I...I think I saw a shade."

"Shades are shy. They don't come near groups of people usually," Talamaya said.

"Aye. Usually." Kersta glanced over at Gallant who was softly snoring. He could fall asleep through about anything.

Argon was awake though, his sword resting on his chest, waiting to protect them if anyone needed his protection.

Kersta sighed and laid back down on her travel mat. "All right. Mexia is protecting us." And she saw two shades moving right outside Mexia's invisible protection shield.

And then one of the shades reached out to her and touched her mind. *"They're not what they seem, my lady. They're more than me, but less than you. They shouldn't exist."*

Kersta sat up on her mat, but there was no shade touching her, just a couple of them disappearing into the fog. Had she dreamt that the shade had shared words with her?

"What is it now?" Talamaya asked, raised up on her elbows on her mat.

Argon was sitting up, fully awake also. "What is wrong?"

Kersta told them what she thought she heard the shade tell her. "It was probably a dream."

"Aye, but thanks for telling us," Talamaya said, "just in case you weren't having just a dream."

Gallant rolled over and patted his bedroll. "Join me for a cuddle, woman, and you will see nay more shades."

Kersta scoffed. "Nay, but I would hear your snoring in my ear all the rest of the night."

"I dinna snore. I keep telling ye that." Gallant closed his eyes.

Talamaya shared a smile with Kersta. Mexia appeared to be asleep this time.

Kersta swore the way Argon was watching her, he wanted to offer a place next to him on his bedroll. Now *that* was a much appealing prospect.

7

That night, Mirabella and Leogane and his party arrived at the healer's hut. The duke hadn't spoken another word to Mirabella, and she'd been just as grateful. If they came under attack by Vladek's men, she would stay with the party, as long as she could. For now, she had every intention of speaking to Justina, to try and discover why Inari called her his niece, but Leogane pulled Mirabella from her horse and guided her into the thatched one-room house without a word. Then he posted guards at the windows and door and headed back outside.

But he didn't allow Justina to go inside with her.

"Send Justina inside," Mirabella said to the guards. She was furious that the duke would stop her from speaking with her maid. Everyone seemed to conspire against her.

"Would you like some mead, my lady?" a woman asked.

Mirabella swung around to find a red-haired woman standing over a kettle, stirring some bubbling liquid. Curls of blue mist rose from the frothing liquid.

Her mouth curved up and the warmth reached all the way to her sparkling green eyes. "Mead, my lady," the woman asked again. She appeared youthful, maybe in her early twenties, yet her voice and actions seemed much older.

"No, thank you," Mirabella said, trying to curb her annoyance with Leogane and put on a good face for the healer who tried to make her feel welcome. "Do you hear much news here about the surrounding region?"

"People come through here from time to time, aye," the woman said and motioned to a wooden chair beside a small round table. "'Tis a dangerous place to live unless you reside in the castle. What is it you wish to know?"

"Do you know anything about Count Vladek?"

The woman's lips curved up even more. "He is a handsome man, about the same age as your duke."

"He is *not* my duke."

Smiling more broadly, the woman nodded, and went back to stirring her broth, or whatever it was.

"Your name? I'm afraid I've been locked up for months in the tower and don't have any gift for—"

"You have many gifts, my lady. You will soon learn to use them."

"I'm a magic user?" Mirabella quickly asked, her voice hushed lest the men outside heard them speak.

The woman's red brows rose.

"Not a magic user? Then what?"

"Your mother was from Racine."

"Where Count Vladek is from?"

"Aye. But he is not related to you. I am Sistani and must tell you that you must not wed Leogane if you wish to make things right between your uncle and you."

"King Inari is *not* my uncle. My brother killed my father and sold me to the king." Besides, Inari had offered her to Leogane also so what the woman said wasn't true.

"Leogane cares not what befell your father or you. Just like your uncle, the duke is a greedy man. He doesn't want you, and yet he has removed you from Castle Mayen. Why? Because Leogane wants the lands and coin that King Inari will bestow upon him. Leogane will take you as a wife, and maybe you will suffer an accident? He will then marry his chief advisor's daughter, the woman he already loves, and have your properties too."

Clenching her teeth, Mirabella tried not to think about Leogane's dislike of her, or his love for another woman. "What about Count Vladek? Would he not gain much for marrying me?"

"He has already told King Inari he doesn't want anything but you. You are of Racine bloodlines. You belong with your people."

She belonged with her own people back home where Argon would rule.

"I don't want Count Vladek's men to attack my escort. I don't want to see any more of his men die."

Sistani didn't say anything, just stirred the contents of her pot.

"Can you get word to him?"

The woman's lips turned up. "Aye."

"Will he...will he listen?"

"Difficult to say. He wishes to please you, but he also wants you. He feels no one will take care of you like one of your own kind."

"My own kind is my brother Argon and the people I left behind. Have you ever seen people such as these?" Mirabella asked the healer.

"Such as?"

"The men who die and leave ashes behind?" Mirabella asked. The healer shook her head.

There was something not quite right about the healer, Mirabella thought. "Have you been here long?"

"Aye, for years."

"You've never encountered these creatures before?" Mirabella asked the woman again.

"I have said no, have I not?"

"Aye, but, well, they seemed to know you." Which was totally made up, but if Mirabella got a rise out of the woman, she could tell if she was in league with them or not.

The woman gave her a smile that didn't reach her eyes this time. "I have never seen them before. I'm sure word has gotten out that I'm the healer for the region."

"Aww, but what could you do for them when they turn to dust? I mean, they don't appear to need a healer."

"I wouldn't know, though I'm sure if they live in this area at all, the word would have reached them about me."

"Uh-huh." Which was true, and the woman was careful not to react in any way that said otherwise. Mirabella still didn't trust the woman. Suffice it to say, Mirabella did have trust issues of late. Who could blame her?

"Are you sure you don't want something to drink, princess?" the healer asked.

"No, I have my flask, thank you."

The door squeaked open, and a guard walked inside. "His Grace wished me to stay inside with you, my lady."

The healer turned her head a little and nodded. "As you wish."

Sinking onto the hard-wooden chair, Mirabella sipped from her own flask. "I want to speak to Justina."

TWO OF HIS men gathered wood for a campfire while others caught game for the meal. Leogane and the rest kept watch while he spoke to Justina. "Tell me about your mistress."

Justina looked back at the hut, as if she were afraid to tell the truth.

His jaw tightened. He couldn't abide anyone being cruel to servants. "You have nothing to fear from the lady. Please tell me what she's like."

"Why she is cruel, my lord. She pulled the wings off a baby bird and killed the poor thing afterwards. She pushed a young boy into a swollen river, and no one could save him before he drowned. She loves nothing, man or beast. Even when governesses would try to teach her anything, she would throw such fits her tutors quit. She has started fires in the castle, escaped so many times that she has to be guarded always. And, I hate to say this about the princess, but..." The woman looked at the ground, and bit her lip, then looked up at Leogane. "Everyone knows she makes up any story she can to suit herself. Blames others for her actions too."

He nodded sympathetically, then crossed his arms and took a deep breath. "Yet you seemed relieved you were leaving Castle Mayen. If it meant serving the lady further, why is this so?"

"That place is a horrible castle to stay at. You saw the way it was, isolated from the rest of the world like a giant prison."

"Was the lady imprisoned in the tower for very long?"

"I wouldn't know."

But she knew about everything else. It seemed odd she would not know about this. "Her father died in a hunting accident, her uncle said. Was that when she was taken to the tower?" He wondered then if that was when the trouble began. A troubled child, angered her father was no longer in charge, or maybe because he'd died.

Before Justina could answer, Erlin, his chief advisor, hurried to speak with him, his face ashen, his posture concerned, his shoulder length black hair disheveled. "Your Grace," he said, "I must speak with you in private."

Leogane said to Justina, "Wait here for me. I have further questions."

She curtseyed deeply, smiling. "Aye, my lord, and I eagerly await your return."

Too eagerly, he thought.

Out of her hearing, he said, "What's the trouble, Lord Erlin?"

"We found the healer dead in the bushes several yards from the cottage. She's redheaded like the woman inside, but I swear the woman we found dead is the healer, and the other, an imposter."

Leogane pulled his sword, and so did Erlin and stormed to the hut. But then thinking better on it, he sheathed his sword, and motioned for his advisor to do the same. Carefully, he pulled the door open, and seeing the princess unharmed he said, "The boar is done. Come join us outside."

She should have done as he told her, but instead, she turned her head toward the campfire outside. "It doesn't smell done to me."

'Twas not the fact she acted contrary to his wishes that perturbed him so, but she seemed to sense things she ought not. Worse, if he didn't get her out of the hut at once before the imposter realized what he intended his men to do...

"I wish to speak with you in private, princess. Does it always have to be a contest of wills between us?" he asked, his voice on edge.

She rose slowly from the chair, and he imagined if she could do so even more slowly, she would. When she neared him, he seized her arm, ignoring her gasp, and pulled her out of the house. He motioned to Erlin to enter.

Already two more of his men were at Erlin's side, and the three rushed in, then slammed the door.

Leogane pulled the princess farther away from the hut, hoping the woman inside wouldn't shriek or that Mirabella wouldn't hear his men's swords cut the woman down. Had the imposter thought to poison him and his men? That's what he assumed.

"What...what's happening?" Mirabella asked, her face stricken.

He realized then, she would guess what was going on. "The woman was an imposter and had murdered the real healer. My men found her dead in the bushes some distance from the hut." Though he hadn't expected the lady's brown eyes to roll back in her head, the color to drain from her cheeks so quickly, or her knees to buckle out from under her, he caught her as soon as she swooned. He couldn't help but notice the softness of her curves resting in his arms, or the sweet fragrance of rosewater that enveloped her like a floral fairy meadow. 'Twas unacceptable that he felt anything for the woman.

Taking his mind off the temptress, he wondered if the woman had no heart, felt nothing for man or beast, why had she fainted dead away? 'Twas not a trick either. He had seen women perform such faints to get his attention or other male admirers', but in those cases, their cheeks remained the same color as before.

He carried her to his bedding and lay her on the blankets next to the fire, caressing her hand and patting it, not sure what else to do.

"Is the lady all right?" Erlin asked, joining him.

"Aye. Is the witch dead?"

"Aye. But you won't believe what happened."

"What?"

"Jeremias stabbed her several times, missing her heart and the woman still didn't die. When I managed to cut off her head, she turned to ashes."

"She was one of them then. One of Count Vladek's people."

"There was something else, Your Grace." Erlin motioned to

the princess. "Jeremias overheard them talking, and that's why he entered the house to stop the conspiracy."

"The princess was going to have all of us murdered in our sleep." Leogane knew the woman wasn't to be trusted, but this was going too far.

Erlin quirked a black brow and folded his arms. "Nay, the princess asked the woman to get a message to the count. Specifically, to tell him not to harm her escort."

"Not to harm us?" Leogane couldn't believe it. If the maid's words were true, the woman was as cold blooded as Vladek's knights.

"Her mother was from Racine. Did you know?"

The duke stood. "She was a magic user?"

Erlin shrugged. "I don't know that everyone from there is. Maybe only the ones who are sent to thwart us and take the lady home with them are. The imposter told the princess you wanted her lands, whereas the count wanted them not. He only wishes the lady because she belongs with her people."

Leogane did not believe the count one bit. Why would anyone give up the lady's lands when they were offered as her dowry? If Vladek wished her so badly, why had he not sought taking her earlier? Something about this stank, like a mongrel dog that had rolled in something dead.

"Anything else?"

"The imposter told the princess that you would take her for your wife, then she would meet with an accident, and you would then marry my daughter, the woman you truly love."

Shaking his head, Leogane paced. "I assume the princess believes it."

Things didn't add up. Why would the princess not want her escort killed, if she was a cold-blooded woman like the maid had said? He glanced over at the woman who watched them, her eyes huge. She hadn't made a move toward them to help with her mistress.

Erlin looked back at her maid, apparently also wondering why the woman wasn't helping with the princess.

"Get me some water." Leogane crouched beside Mirabella. He couldn't ignore the fact she'd tried to get word to the count's men not to harm them.

Erlin hurried back with a bucket of cold water, while his men either cooked the boar they killed, or served on guard duty.

Taking a cloth from his pack, the duke wetted it and wiped the princess's face. Immediately she tried to sit up but held her head and lay back down.

He watched her, noticing at once the color had not returned to her face. "Are you all right, princess?"

Her eyes filled with tears, and she looked away.

"She murdered the healer, my lady." Then he lied, figuring it was the truth, though he didn't know for certain. "She intended to poison us, all but you, before we bedded down for the night."

Mirabella closed her eyes and tears dribbled down her cheeks.

He patted her hand and stood. Was she upset her message would not get to Count Vladek? "The boar will be done soon, princess. Then we'll sleep and get an early start in the morn." He motioned to Erlin. "Watch her."

"Aye, Your Grace. Like a hawk." He winked.

When the meal was done, the princess would not eat, rolled onto her side, and pulled Leogane's blankets around herself. After he'd eaten, the duke carried her inside the hut, and lay her in the bed.

Opening her eyes, she stared at him while he pulled the blanket up to her chin.

"You will sleep in here where 'tis more comfortable. There is only one bed, no sense in letting it go to waste. We will find no dwelling for the next night."

She nodded and closed her eyes, while he, the maid, and two of his men slept inside. He didn't trust the maid when normally he would have had her stay with Mirabella in the hut. The other knights took turns guarding the hut or sleeping outside.

Twice in the middle of the night, the princess cried out, the men grumbled, and the duke quieted her fears. Twice more she walked in her sleep, though at first, he thought she was trying to escape, then realized she was sleepwalking like his sister did when she was overly tired at night.

The next morning his men served porridge, and the party remounted their horses for another day's journey, only this time Leogane intended to ride much longer, or at this rate, they'd never make it to the beach and his anchored ship.

What with the restless sleep the princess had, she looked half asleep, her dark hair braided, but half of her silken tresses undone. She still seemed distraught, incapable of noticing she hadn't properly fixed her hair. Her maid never offered to help her. Plus, Mirabella had waved away the morning meal.

Leogane glanced back at the maid, who watched the woods, probably fearing more attacks, but he couldn't help feeling annoyed that the woman, who was being paid to serve the princess, wasn't doing her job. When they stopped to eat, he would insist she braid the princess's hair, and he wouldn't allow Mirabella to miss another meal.

For now though, he kept an eye on the princess, who appeared ready to fall asleep at any moment. Twice she nodded off, and he reached out to wake her, not wanting her to fall from her horse and risk injury.

The third time, he reached over, and pulled her from her saddle, startling her.

"What—"

"You're falling asleep, and we can't afford to stop after we've only just begun our journey. Rest."

Jeremias rode up from behind, his blond hair flying, and he grabbed her horse's reins, then dropped back.

Mirabella sat stiffly in the duke's arms for a good half hour, then slowly sank against him. The next thing he knew, her head was planted against his chest, and she was sleeping soundly. He told himself he had no feelings for the woman, yet he had never held a lady so close, and he couldn't help but enjoy the feel of her against his body, fitting nicely like the soft leather gloves he wore when he hunted with his bow.

Erlin rode up beside him. "She's like your sister at night, eh?"

"Sleepwalking. Aye. The man who weds her will have to tie her to his bed if he wants her to remain there."

Erlin laughed. "I know you have an obligation to the king, and Leetonia understands this as well. Think nothing of it if you decide to take the princess for your wife."

Leogane took a deep breath. "I do not know what to think of the woman, but she is not the one for me. If she is a magic user, she should be with her people."

"If she is a magic user, why doesn't she use her powers?"

Leogane looked over at his advisor, realizing at once the gravity of the situation. "Did the healer imposter fight you?"

"No, it was as if she were ordered to be a sacrificial lamb."

He shook his head. "I don't understand. Unless these people aren't magic users."

"Or unless they don't want to reveal their powerful use of magic, just yet."

"Something's not right. I can't pinpoint what, but something's not right." Leogane turned to his advisor. "When we were in the hut, could you smell if the boar was finished cooking?"

"I was trying to kill the imposter."

"Aye."

"Why do you ask, Your Grace?"

Erlin had been his devoted advisor once the duke's father had died from a fever. He trusted him with his life, never having kept any secrets from him, yet now, Leogane couldn't reveal what concerned him most about the lady. He shook his head. "'Tis nothing."

His advisor looked at the lady sleeping in the duke's arms, and he was sure Erlin figured the lady was either some sort of sorcerer, or something they knew not what, just as he suspected.

Erlin looked ahead and waved his arm at the cliff faces banded in green, gold, and red strips of clay as if a master painter colored the whole cliffs in his spare time. "We are nearly to the pass."

"Aye, and I suspect the dark knights will again attack us there."

Jagged outcroppings of rocks covered with bushy firs provided perfect brigand hiding places, while they waited for the unsuspecting to travel through.

Leogane's scouts turned back to report before they ventured into the pass. "Your Grace," one of the men said. "We heard nothing. Shall we venture into the pass?"

Mirabella lifted her head from Leogane's chest and shook it. "Nay, they are waiting for us there." She pointed to the right of the pass. "Behind those rocks that look like my father's advisor's enormous beak."

His men stared at the woman in disbelief, and Leogane wondered the same thing. "How do you know this, princess?"

"Did you not hear them?" she asked, her brows raised and her eyes wide with disbelief. "They were counting our numbers, having assumed we might have lost some of our men in the earlier battle. Did you not hear them?"

He didn't know what to think about her now. "Could you tell how many were there?"

"Three, I think. Unless there are more who didn't speak. But I heard three distinctive voices."

"We can easily take them if there are only three of them," the scout said.

"What if she's wrong?" Erlin asked, his voice concerned.

What he didn't say was what if the woman had lied?

"You, Jeremias, and Kirszner stay with the princess." Leogane would have included the maid, but he didn't fear that the maid would run away or that these dark knights would care anything about her. "Guard her well." He didn't want anyone grabbing the princess and taking off with her.

"Aye, my lord." Erlin helped her from Leogane's horse, but instead of putting her on her own horse, he kept her on his saddle.

She objected at once. "Shouldn't—"

"I will protect you better this way."

Leogane nodded. His advisor knew his thoughts well without having to speak them. He motioned to the rest of his men. "A force of at least three men are at that first outcropping of rocks to the right. We'll send them back to the devil from where they came."

With his sword raised, he led his men to battle, and hoped the lady had not sent them into a trap.

8

M irabella wanted to protect her escort in the worst way. But now voices were swirling around in her head.

She has told them we are here!

She is to be one of us!

She will be the death of us!

Desiring with a vengeance to know if Erlin heard the voices too, she crushed that notion, figuring that no one seemed to hear anything that she did. She thought at first it was that the canyon walls caused the men's voices to echo off them, though there were no echoes, just the initial comments.

Jeremias and Kirszner watched behind them, while Erlin kept his attention focused on Leogane and the rest of the men.

The duke rode into battle, his gleaming sword catching the sun's rays as he held it high, his tall stature and broad shoulders imposing.

Kill the duke and the rest will give her up!

"No!" she shouted.

"What's the matter, my lady?" Erlin asked.

"They...they want to kill the duke."

Erlin chuckled. "They are welcome to try."

She held her arms around herself, the chill in the air seeming to intensify.

"Do you hear them speaking still?"

She shook her head, having said too much already.

"Did you smell the boar cooking outside the healer's hut?"

"'Twas a strong scent. Anyone would have smelled it."

"Aye."

But the way the duke's advisor answered her, she did not think he believed her.

"How long have you been able to hear so acutely, princess?"

She didn't speak for fear of incriminating herself.

"You seem surprised that you have this ability that no one else seems to have. I would venture to say you are gaining some unique abilities as you grow older. Can you do magic?"

She opened her mouth to argue with him, but just then three men dressed in chain mail and the familiar black tunics emblazoned with a red rose jumped out at the duke from behind the colorful clay rocks. Two swung swords at him, but when the rest of the duke's escort caught up with them, they easily cut down Vladek's men.

"They thought there were fewer of us left," she said under her breath.

"Us?"

"Of you, the duke and his men," she quickly corrected.

"Is that why there were fewer in number this time? They didn't think the duke and his men would be so...invincible?"

She thought there was a hint of threat in Erlin's words, but when she studied him, he only smiled back.

For some strange reason, maybe because the duke's advisor had a daughter most likely near her age, maybe because he acted as her guard, but was not mean to her like the one's King Inari had posted for her, she felt the urge to tell this man things

she'd allowed to fester deep inside her for the past several
months. Whether he believed her or not, it didn't matter.

"My brother killed my father," she said, softly. "He said it was
a hunting accident but I was there. I saw what had happened. I
witnessed my brother nocking his arrow and aiming for my
father, deliberately loosing it, and striking my father down. Zane
didn't see me observe the murder, at least I don't think. Before I
could get word to my other brother Argon, Zane had me bound
and gagged and shipped off. I finally ended up at the castle here
and have been locked up there ever since." What would it matter
if she told Erlin who would no doubt disbelieve her anyway? At
least she would say her mind.

"Hunting accidents happen all the time, my lady." Though
Erlin spoke gently, his blue eyes continued to watch her as if to
see her response.

"Aye, a planned and executed, cold-blooded hunting accident. I don't know who my mother's family was. She died when I
was born. But I have never heard of King Inari." She looked at
Erlin to see his response to that.

His eyes turned hard, as if annoyed she would be so
confused about what had happened. That she would condemn
her brother for unspeakable things. "Are you sure you don't have
it all wrong, my lady? Surely 'twas a hunting accident, nothing
more."

"Why was I locked in the tower then?"

"I assume His Majesty did so to protect you."

She gave a short derisive laugh, then listened to Leogane
giving orders to his men. As before, they examined the bodies,
lifting helms high, where only powdered ashes remained,
spilling from the iron masks, scattering on the breeze.

"If King Inari had some other reason to keep you at Castle
Mayen, pray tell what it was," Erlin said.

She watched as Leogane looked back at her, and seeing she

was still with his advisor, he remounted his horse and spoke again to his men. "I tell you I've never heard of King Inari before. My brother Zane must have sold me to the king. I was locked in the tower on the island so I couldn't escape before he gave me to Leogane or Vladek for his own purposes."

"But you had free rein of the castle and of the servants."

"Of my chamber, you mean. And no, I was in charge of no one."

Erlin shifted uneasily in his saddle.

"Come now, you cannot say the man who says he is my uncle has ever mentioned me before to Leogane."

Clearing his throat, Erlin said, "He hasn't, I have to admit."

"Aye, well, see? I'm telling the truth."

Leogane galloped back to them, sweat dribbling from his furrowed brow, his horse kicking up the dust. "We move forward through the pass now, but I want you to ride up ahead with me, Princess Mirabella."

So Leogane believed her now. She wasn't sure if this was a good thing or bad. Pursing her lips, she didn't want to be used by the duke, then cast aside when he didn't need her any longer. Then she sighed deeply. She didn't want her escort hurt either. For now, she would aid the duke and his men, but later, she would be the sliver in his sword hand that he would soon want to be rid of. She had been watching and listening for any sign of her brother, but she sensed nothing, and she feared he might have come to harm at the hand of these knights. Unless they only attacked her escort.

Jeremias brought her horse, and once she had mounted him, she and Leogane moved slowly through the pass, while she listened for any sound, any whispered words. "I hear none but your men speaking about my strange ability and how worried they are that I might attack you when you sleep."

Leogane turned and gave Erlin a look. The wordless communication spurred his advisor to return to the men who followed them some distance behind.

She heard Erlin telling the men to cease their prattle, making her smile, gladdened that she was not the only one who was told to stop talking. She glanced at the duke who watched her with a mixture of fascination and concern. Then he looked back at his men. Erlin kicked his horse and rejoined them, just slightly behind Mirabella's horse, probably to ensure she was protected in the event she didn't hear anyone ahead, and they were attacked anyway.

Their horses' hooves clip-clopped on the stone floor of the canyon, almost deafening as it echoed off the canyon walls.

Every time they drew close to an outcropping of rocks, they paused and waited for her to tell them if the area was clear. It should have made her proud she could accomplish something no one else could, something worthy of praise. But the men seemed uneasy of her ability which confirmed the healer imposter's words that Mirabella would be better off with her own kind.

She wondered then if everyone in Racine had her ability. Though she only wanted to rejoin her own people.

The canyon walls of the long narrow pass stretched so high they were taller than the castle towers at Castle Mayen, nearly blocking out the sun in places. They finally exited the canyon pass and saw the golden sphere of the sun dipping behind the mountains and a sparkling blue lake beckoned to her. Instantly, she remembered how years ago she had picnicked with several maids near a lake such as this. Immediately she drew her horse closer.

"Lake Orchy," Leogane informed her. "'Tis said a giant from beyond the mountains of the Five Sisters of Xerxes stomped his foot in anger, attempting to squash an annoying bird and left the crater. He broke his ankle and cried for half a year, filling the hole with his tears."

"'Tis salty then?" she asked.

"Nay. The rains over the centuries have diluted it until it became a freshwater lake." He smiled.

Did he think her foolish for believing the tale?

She jumped down from her horse, crouched at the water's edge, and stuck her hand in. The water felt warm and silky against her skin. "'Tis warm."

"Aye, they say underwater vents feed warmth into the water."

"Can I bathe?"

"Nay."

She frowned at him, feeling filthy from the dirt kicked up by their horses. She imagined her face and her hair were covered in dust. "But no more of Vladek's men are in the area."

The duke raised his dark brows. "But my men are."

"They can turn their backs."

Leogane turned to his advisor. "Have the men prepare camp."

"Aye, my lord." Erlin moved in the direction of the men and gave the orders.

Some of the men began setting up tents, others providing security, while others started to build the campfires.

Turning to face her, Leogane said, "We have no idea what might live in the water."

She grabbed a pack off her horse. The water was too inviting, but she had to agree Leogane could be right. "You could be nicer toward me."

"I was thinking the same of you. It would be nice if for once when I told you to do something, or that you should not do something, you would obey me without argument."

"Would Erlin's daughter be so complacent?"

"I think the term is agreeable. And aye, that she would. The perfect wife." He stalked off, giving one last order to Erlin. "Watch her."

"You would think he doesn't trust me," she said to Erlin while she removed the satin ribbons from her hair.

"What makes you think that, princess?"

"He always has you guard me. I would not run off. 'Tis too dangerous."

"He wants no one to seize you and take you away."

She unwound her braids, more of the hair undone than braided. "What about you? Surely you would love to ensure your daughter and not I would wed the duke."

"I wish what is best for His Grace. If he decides he wishes you instead—"

"I want him not," Mirabella snapped back. No pretend uncle would decide this for her.

Folding his arms, Erlin's gray eyes studied her. "Aye, but 'tis not your decision. What do you know of Vladek?"

"Nothing. I've never met him."

"And you want to marry him because?"

"That is an idiotic question. I don't want him. But your lord doesn't want me either. 'Tis as simple as that."

"Vladek won't be happy you're warning us about his men."

She sat down on the grass and pulled off her leather shoes and hose, mulling over that notion. "I would not do otherwise. There's something not right about him. I wouldn't sacrifice your men to his."

She washed her hands, feet, and her face in the lake. Then she returned to the tent and changed into something fresh while she heard Erlin talking to Leogane as she curled up in the blankets she would sleep on this night.

"SHE BELIEVES, my lord, that her brother murdered her father on a hunting expedition and sold her to King Inari. That he isn't even her uncle. Another matter, though. She seems to hear what the rest of us cannot."

"Aye." Leogane frowned at his advisor. "If she isn't the king's niece..."

"I don't know what to think. She didn't know her mother's family. Mayhap he is her uncle on her mother's side. About her sensitive hearing, I was close enough to you when you spoke to the maid about the princess. Though she was in the healer's hut at the time..."

Leogane glanced at Mirabella, her eyes shut tight, her breathing shallow in sleep. "You think she might have overheard what the maid said?"

"I think 'tis a possibility. I've never met anyone who could hear like she does, only the wolves and cheetaurs can hear like that. You asked me earlier if I could smell the meat cooking when I was in the hut with the imposter. Why did you ask this of me, my lord?"

"She said the meat was not done cooking. I knew she spoke the truth but could not understand how she would know. She had not seen us spit the meat. She wouldn't have known how long it was hanging above the flames."

"She assumed it hadn't been long enough?"

Shaking his head, Leogane glanced back at the fire. "Nay, I don't think so."

"So you're saying?"

The duke straightened his back and looked at the figure half buried in blankets. "Her sense of smell is more acute as well."

s soon as it was light out, Argon and the dwarf and the women had a quick meal and then headed to the wetlands.

"I'm going to try and levitate one of you at a time. Using my magic to protect us last night, I can't do more than one," Mexia said.

"I thought you couldn't use your magic that soon again after using it to protect us last night," Talamaya said.

"I didn't think so either, but it seems I've grown more powerful. I dinna feel drained of my abilities at all this morning," Mexia said. "But there's something else. I feel...Derek is with me."

"From so far away?" Kersta asked.

"Aye."

"'Tis your woman's yearning for him, naught more," Gallant grumbled.

Mexia sighed. "Nay. We are mages—connected for all time, so it seems. And mayhap connected against vast distances as well. In any case, I feel him with me. 'Tis possible he is working his magic through me, empowering me."

"That would be welcome," Talamaya said. "He does not want to lose you, so that is also understandable."

"I agree." Then Kersta looked around at the ground again covered in pine needles shed here for decades, she figured. "Leogane and his party didn't go this way, did they? They couldn't have made it across the wetlands on horseback if there's quicksand here." She quickly examined the map again. "There was another path—just a tiny trail. Darn it. It was getting dark, and I couldn't see it. We took the wrong path."

"How long would it take to backtrack?" Argon asked.

"Too long." Kersta was glad Argon didn't seem angry with her for making the mistake. She was angry enough with herself.

Argon rubbed her shoulder. "None of us had seen the trail. 'Tis not your fault."

Gallant snorted. "If I had been reading the map—"

"Did you see the trail?" Argon asked, just as gruffly, sticking up for Kersta when she was feeling just awful about this.

Gallant shook his head.

"I'm sending all of you over," Mexia said. "But just one at a time so I can be assured I won't drop anyone into the swamp." Before Gallant was ready, she levitated him and carried him across the swampy area. "I'll set you down right at the edge."

Gallant cried out. "Ye could have warned me, woman!"

Kersta smiled a little because he was always so fearsome, and nothing seemed to faze him.

He was nearly to the other side when Kersta saw bubbles in the water below him. "There's something in the water."

Gallant readied his hammer. "Hurry it up, woman!" Now he was worried!

Though Kersta understood how he felt, she felt it for him, she also knew Mexia couldn't hurry any faster or she'd drop him. And then Mexia had him over the shore on the other side and as soon as she set him down, a green, hairy beast of a man came up of the water, a trident-like spear in its clawed hand and headed for Gallant. The dwarf struck the swamp beast twice with his hammer, the creature falling back, not even having time to strike out against the fierce dwarf. With a bloodied shoulder and chest, the creature dove back into the water and disappeared.

"Hurry, send another person over," Gallant said, no doubt wanting reinforcements on his side and Kersta agreed.

This time Mexia sent Talamaya. No more creatures emerged and Kersta figured the swamp creature believed it couldn't fight them and win. Then Talamaya was on the other bank and Kersta was next. "There are more of them. More bubbles I mean. Get ready!" Kersta called out.

Though she didn't know if the bubbles were from something else, like turtles or fish, anything that wasn't predatory in nature —at least toward them.

Mexia lifted Kersta and began sending her to the other side. It wasn't an easy task. Mexia had to concentrate and chill bumps prickled Kersta's skin as she made the slow passage airborne across the swamp. She liked to have her feet on solid ground or while she was sitting securely on the back of a horse. Even riding a dragon was enough to give her chills. Meanwhile, Argon had his sword out and was prepared to battle anything that came out of the green muck to fight Mexia and him.

Kersta was glad Mexia could use her mage skills to do this, but when Mexia had to levitate Kersta before, she'd felt the same apprehension. If one of the swamp creatures attacked Mexia, she'd lose her concentration and Kersta would fall into the swamp.

Three more of the swamp creatures emerged, coming to join in the fight. Two of them headed for Mexia this time as if they knew she couldn't fight them. Not while she was using her magic to move Kersta across the swamp and Kersta was only halfway to the other side. She realized now, the other one hadn't left to lick his wounds but had gone back in to get reinforcements!

The third creature went after Kersta, jumping up to knock her into the algae-covered water.

Kersta hit him in the head with her staff and knocked him back into the swamp. He went under. Had she killed him? Stunned him?

Then two more creatures emerged from the water and went after Talamaya and Gallant and they shoved their tridents at them, meaning to skewer the princess and the dwarf with the sharp barbs. The princess swung her staff and Gallant, his war hammer at them, connecting with their tridents, both of the creatures losing their weapons with the strong blows. They dove back into the swamp to make a hasty retreat.

Mexia was trying to get Kersta to the other side, while Argon swung his sword at the two creatures, one trying to reach Mexia. They had long, raking claws and sharp, jagged teeth that they bared at Mexia and Argon, swiping at them with their dagger-like claws at the same time, thrusting with their tridents. They hissed and growled and bit at each other as if to say the prey in front of them was their own and stay away.

The creature targeting Mexia managed to slash her arm and she lost her concentration on the levitation spell. Kersta fell.

"Kersta!" Argon shouted in panic.

Kersta's heart was in her throat as she splashed into the water and sank beneath the murky surface. Panicked, she clawed her way out of the brackish water, praying Mexia's wound was something they could heal. And hoping nothing would attack Kersta before she could make it out of the swamp!

She finally made it to the surface and caught her breath. She saw Gallant and Talamaya fighting off three of the beasts and heard fighting behind her. She didn't have time to look. She had to swim or get to her feet on a sandbar and reach the shore as quickly as she could.

Then she felt a clawed hand grab her ankle as she was swimming, crawling on sand, trying to make it the rest of the way across the swamp. Her heart was pounding furiously as she kicked the creature with her free, booted foot, connecting with its head that felt like a big, flesh-covered coconut.

It grunted and then growled, and she knew she was in trouble! But he was under the moss-covered water still and she couldn't hit the creature with the staff if she couldn't see it.

She felt a slice to her ankle. Teeth? Claws? She kicked again, though the water slowed her actions and even though she struck something with her boot, it didn't have the impact she needed. She swam away again, her skin burning where the creature, whatever it was, had cut her.

Then she found a sandbar of sorts and hurried to clamber up on top of it, grateful she was out of the swampy water. But she still had more swamp to travel through and Mexia and the prince were still fighting others behind her. Then she remembered her cloak and turned it so that she was instantly invisible. Moving through the swamp again, the land giving way, she was in the water, swimming, which meant the creatures could see the movement in the water and surmise she was making it. Though she would confuse them, and they wouldn't find her easily, she hoped.

Then she felt movement behind her, and she worried a swamp creature was trying to reach her. She felt a metal object strike her—a trident, and she tried not to call out and giveaway her position completely. She was suddenly on her knees again, another bit of higher land, and this time she could finally leap for the bank where Talamaya and Gallant fought more of the swamp creatures. Three of them. And Kersta planned to enter the battle.

That was until a creature struck her from behind, knocking her to the side. He was swinging his trident, trying to connect with her wherever she was. Unfortunately, he'd hit her, knew it because he'd met something solid—her shoulder, which hurt like the devil—and knocked her into the water where her body created a loud splash—no!

Panic filled her as she clawed at the water to reach the surface.

But then she came up out of the water, swinging at the swamp creature that was targeting her and struck him hard in the chest. He went down and disappeared into the swamp.

She hurried the rest of the way out of the swamp. She coughed and Gallant frowned, the other swamp creatures gone now. "Is that ye, woman?"

"Aye." A little battered and aching to high heaven. Kersta glanced back at Mexia and Argon.

Two swamp creatures floated on top of the water near the opposite bank where Argon and Mexia had dealt with them. Kersta gave a relieved breath they were still all right.

Before Mexia could levitate Argon, he swept her up in his arms and raced across the swamp. Mexia's arm was bleeding and Kersta turned her cloak visible and hurriedly got her healing pack out. Argon was sinking into the water like she had, the water deep in parts of it, then getting purchase on a sandy shoal, moving as quickly as he could. Kersta's heart was about to give out she was so worried that the swamp things would attack them as they were trying to cross the swamp, and no one could reach them to fight the beasts off unless they joined them in the water. Which she didn't want to do again. Though she would if she had to.

"You've been injured," Talamaya said to Kersta.

"Aye, easily healed, I'm sure, once I take care of Mexia." Since Mexia was an expert healer.

And then two more swamp creatures came out of the water and Kersta, Talamaya, and Gallant rushed forth to fight them while Argon reached the shore with Mexia. The two creatures went down and disappeared into the water. Kersta swore they were different ones every time, and she thought they had killed the others, or stunned them so they couldn't fight any longer.

But when Gallant lunged at another swamp beast, the dwarf ended up in quicksand and Argon and Talamaya grabbed his arms and pulled him free. Talamaya and Gallant fell back on the ground and Argon pulled the princess to her feet.

"Thanks for carrying me across the swamp," Mexia said to Argon as Talamaya took the healing pack Kersta had opened up and began to apply the herbs and cloth to fight the infection already spreading throughout Mexia's wound.

"You would never have made it on your own, if you'd had to fight those creatures and transport me to the other side," Argon said.

Kersta realized he was right. And she thought—if he wasn't a prince on a quest of his own—he would have been perfect to take on quests with them as they had done in the past.

But then Gallant brushed off his wet, algae-covered clothes and frowned at Kersta. "Mayhap 'tis you who needs spectacles to read the map."

She felt like he did about her wet clothes. Everyone but Talamaya had taken a soaking in the mossy water.

Once Talamaya had used the healing herbs and bandage on Mexia's arm, Mexia worked on Kersta's cut ankle. "Claw marks."

And Kersta could have felt the effect of infection too if they hadn't done something quickly about it. Once Mexia had used her healing magic on Kersta, she frowned at her. "You're still in pain."

"Bruises."

Mexia ran her hands over Kersta's shoulder, and she sighed

with relief. She'd never thought she would like being a mage—not all people trusted them—but she sure wished she had Mexia's gift of healing. "Can you heal yourself now?"

"Aye." Mexia looked down at her arm and it was already healed. "Well, it looks like your healing pack did the trick."

But Kersta didn't believe it. The healing pack took longer to heal their injuries than Mexia's healing powers. She wondered if somehow Derek had aided Mexia from afar. "Do you think Prince Derek has had a hand in this?"

Mexia frowned. "I would not think he could help with his healing powers all the way from Langdon."

"You don't think he's on his way here to protect you?" Talamaya asked.

"We were taken hostage. I don't see how he would know where we are."

"True." Kersta reached over and pulled some moss out of Gallant's beard.

He raised a brow and pulled some out of her hair.

She desperately needed a bath to wash the moss off her skin and out of her hair. At least it was warm on the island, or they'd be freezing.

They quickly headed on their way to find Leogane and his party and Kersta was hoping they'd locate them soon. After walking for some time, Kersta looked at the map again and said, "We are nearly to a healer's hut." She ignored Gallant's comments about her map reading issues, though she did feel guilty that she had mislead them to the place they had been trying to avoid.

"Aye, but did Leogane travel that way too?" Gallant asked, one bushy brow raised.

"He did," Argon said. "We've just come across another path and we're seeing horses' droppings again."

"See? I couldn't see them last night. Could you?" Kersta

asked Gallant.

"I wouldna have made the mistake of taking the wrong path in the first place," Gallant said.

"There was a fight here." Talamaya pointed to the remains of a woman inside the hut. All that was left were her clothes and ashes. "She is like the others. Turned to dust."

"So not all the ones who are here are Vladek's men," Mexia said. "That is good to know."

They continued traveling along the path, finding a few more dark knights' armor and tunics filled with ashes until they saw a rocky pass.

"I don't like the looks of this." Talamaya glanced up at the red canyon walls. "This is too much like some of the places we've traveled before where the cheetaurs blended in with their surroundings."

"Do you see a vision of them?" Kersta asked.

"Nay, but I just don't like the narrow passage and high rocky cliffs on either side. It's perfect for an ambush." Talamaya and Gallant nevertheless led the way.

They found even more dark knight remains along the way.

"Leogane must have been through here and fought these men," Kersta whispered to Argon. "I'm glad they seem to be victorious in every encounter."

"Aye. He has good warriors with him," Argon agreed.

"Like us," Kersta said.

Argon smiled. "Aye, which is why I hired you."

Kersta scoffed. "We *hired* you and you *kidnapped* us."

They moved swiftly through the pass, seeing glimpses of cheetaurs up on the cliffs, but she thought they wouldn't jump that far down to attempt to feast on them. At least she hoped they wouldn't.

∾

ARGON WAS hopeful they were gaining on Leogane and his men, believing the swamp path had cut down the distance they'd had to travel by leaps and bounds. He was also glad they were beyond the swamps. It was bad enough they had to fight these knights all the time, but the swamps could have been just as deadly if Mexia hadn't been able to move some of her companions across them.

He noted that the dark knights had avoided the swamps. There had been no sign of their dispatched bodies there and he wondered if they had stayed on the right path after Leogane and his men. "Your decision to go through the swamps was the best one you could have made," he told Kersta.

"Thank you. After seeing where we are now, I think so too. The horses' droppings are fresher, do you not think?" she asked, sounding glad she'd made the mistake and it had turned out for the best for them. "We are catching up to them, I believe."

"Aye. But they are still on—" Argon heard a horse nickering just beyond the pass where it opened into the woods again.

"Horses," Talamaya whispered. "Dark knights' horses. Ones that are now riderless. We will use them if they'll allow us."

"The dark knights are dead. They have no say in the matter," Gallant said.

Talamaya shook her head. "I meant if the horses will allow us to ride them. They may not accept our kind. They may only allow the dark knights to ride them."

When they emerged from the pass, they saw only two of the dark knights' horses, both pawing at the grass beside the path and nibbling on it. That was still better than no horses at all.

"We will ride double and hope to catch another couple of horses on our way." Talamaya reached out to the horses in a consoling way, her voice soft. The horses nickered at her and didn't seem to be afraid, thank the heavens. She ran her hand over their muzzles.

"But you won't be able to fight as well with two riders seated on a horse," Argon warned.

"Then you can walk. I'll ride with the princess," Gallant said, whether Talamaya wished it or not, though she didn't seem to mind.

"I will run alongside you. We must hurry." Argon was glad they at least had two horses. Even with him running beside them, they should be able to make better time than with all of them walking on foot.

"Can you do that?" Kersta climbed onto the saddle of the other horse. "We can't afford to lose you. Nor can your sister."

"Aye, I can do it." Much better than Gallant, Argon imagined.

Mexia joined Kersta and they rode together, following behind Talamaya and Gallant.

Argon ran in endurance trials with his soldiers, though several often said they were supposed to stand and fight, not run for survival so they could flee in battle. Which had always amused him. Whether they ran toward the battle or away from it, training had been well worth it as his soldiers could attest to. Sometimes it was the time to fight, and other times, they had to flee, regroup, and try again another day. For now, he was truly glad he was in good enough shape to do this.

Kersta kept looking back at him, her expression worried. But with the dwarf's short legs, he couldn't keep up after the horses, and the women most likely didn't have the stamina—he didn't think—to run long distances after the horses either. Argon would manage as long as he needed to.

Then he heard horses headed their way and he thought it odd that when they were in a fight with the dark knights, the knights were always on foot. But it appeared Leogane's men, who were on horseback, had fought dark knights also on horseback.

But the riders couldn't fight well doubled up and Gallant and

Kersta quickly dismounted while Talamaya and Mexia fought the dark knights from horseback. The women were amazing. Argon's army had female warriors in their ranks, but none that were royalty. Aye, his sister could use a sword to defend herself, but she couldn't take down hoards like these women could.

The good news was that these knights were all on horseback and though that gave those of them on foot a harder time, they fought them until the horses reared up to unseat their riders, or they knocked the knights to the ground and finished them off.

When the last of the dark knights was dead, each of the companions and Argon had their own horse, and extras, if they needed them. "Let's go."

They raced off at a quicker pace now that the women didn't have to walk the horses so Argon could keep up at a runner's pace. Maybe now they had a chance to catch up to Leogane and Mirabella. But what kind of a fight would they be in then?

Argon had considered Leogane might want to dispatch him so Leogane could keep Mirabella and whatever dowry King Inari had offered him. And it appeared Leogane's numbers had not decreased since they'd begun this journey.

NOT LONG AFTER they got on the road again, Leogane and his men were in a fight with the dark knights, but no one had a spare sword for Mirabella to use. She would do anything to stop these knights. "They won't hurt me," she said. At least she didn't think so. But the way these knights came at them in hoards, she knew she had to help Leogane and his men. She'd decided after the last battle that whatever these things were that Count Vladek conjured up, she didn't want any part of being with him.

"Nay, lass, stay inside the circle. They could grab you and carry you off. I cannot allow it," Leogane shouted as he killed another of the dark knights and the horse ran off, the knight falling to the ground dead.

But then she heard fighting further away. And she heard her brother say, "Kersta, watch out!"

"Thanks, Argon. We make a good team, do we not?" a woman said, her voice cheerful.

"If ye think to be adding him to the party permanently, dinna," a man said, his voice sounding like a dwarf's, husky, darkly gruff. "'Tis his sister he wishes to save, naught more. And let me tell ye—" The man grunted.

Then Mirabella heard more bashing and assumed the dwarf was armed with a war hammer. But who were these people with her brother? Why didn't she hear any of her brother's men speaking to Argon instead?

"...these mountains of gold he offered, he doesna have. Unless he takes over his princedom and who knows how well that will go. What will he use? A handful of sailors who he wouldn't even bring on this journey? Instead, we have to fight his battles? Bah!" the dwarf said again.

So her brother had hired mercenaries? And the one was a woman? Kersta?

"He only has to pay *you*," another woman said. "The rest of us do not need his gold."

Another woman? Her brother would surely be killed! But why would the women help him for naught? It didn't make any sense that they would be so well off that they could risk their lives to rescue Mirabella. Though she appreciated it.

"Argon!" Mirabella called out, then thought better of it. What if she distracted her brother from the fight he was in now and he died because of her?

"Is that fighting we hear coming from the north?" Leogane asked, striking at another dark knight.

"Aye, my good brother. He has come for me, to rescue me. He

will take me home." But Mirabella realized that Zane had taken the treasury when he took over the princedom while Argon had been sent by her father as an emissary to make peace with the neighboring Miramar princedom. Unless Argon had the money to pay their army and take over, he wouldn't have the forces he needed to defeat Zane. Where would Mirabella and Argon go then? At least they had the Duchess and could hopefully sail somewhere to safety.

"You have not mentioned you have another brother," Leogane said, fighting yet another knight.

"Argon knows the truth. That Inari is not our uncle. That Zane has taken the princedom from him. Argon is the rightful ruler. Besides, I already told your advisor about my other brother. I would have thought he would have told you also."

Leogane killed another of the dark knights and then they seemed to fade into the dark woods, into the mist again.

"Do we wait for her brother?" Erlin asked.

"Aye," Mirabella said.

"If we wait here, we might very well have to fight more of these creatures. We must continue on our trek to the beach," Leogane said. "He can catch up to us there."

"Nay, we must wait for my brother and his...forces. All of us would be safer if we fight together." Mirabella hoped her brother had substantial forces. She hadn't even thought about what would happen if Leogane decided he wanted to keep her and fight her brother for her.

She would fight Leogane to stay rooted to this place until her brother and his party reached them though. Not only because she knew they would add warriors to their numbers, but also because she was afraid her brother didn't have too many fighters with him, and he needed *their* aid.

Leogane seemed to ponder the notion.

"If you do this for me, I will be forever grateful and I will go with you willingly." There. She said it. As much as she hadn't wanted to. Once her brother was here for her, Leogane would have no claim to her. But at least Argon could corroborate her story and convince Leogane she was not worth the trouble. The other problem she saw was that they were headed to the wrong side of the island and not to the Duchess, but Leogane's ship.

LEOGANE DESPERATELY WANTED to get Mirabella out of these woods and to safety. Not because he believed the dark knights would kill her, but because he was certain they wanted to take her away and hand her over to whatever vile creature Count Vladek was who could control these knights. On the other hand, he heard the worry in her voice, and he assumed she felt her brother didn't have a strong enough force to fight with. He'd heard a steel sword striking against steel, a hammer clunking against swords and he thought they had a dwarf in their party. The others gave him pause. He swore they sounded like staffs, but a wooden staff would never hold up against steel swords. He wondered how Mirabella would know the ones who were fighting were her brother and his men. Maybe those fighting some manner of being—the dark knights possibly—were centaurs or some other hospitable creature instead.

Though if it was her brother and his men, they could bolster Argon's numbers.

"How do you know your brother and his men are out there and it isn't just the guards who served King Inari from the castle?" Or someone else. Argon had the notion that it possibly was the guards leaving the castle because they no longer had to guard the tower and they were returning to the mainland, though he wondered where their ship was.

Mirabella stared at Leogane in disbelief. "Could you not

hear..." She hesitated to speak as if she feared giving herself away. "I heard one of his party calling out his name."

"I must have been too busy fighting to have heard the exchange." But Leogane wondered if she'd only imagined it or if she'd truly heard her brother's name called out.

"I saw his ship, the Duchess, anchored off the other side of the island from my tower window," she finally admitted.

Leogane's jaw dropped. She knew her brother was coming to rescue her this whole time? "You couldn't have told me this sooner?" He scoffed. "We will wait."

But he realized then he could have trouble with her brother if Leogane decided to take Mirabella as his wife.

His advisor and the rest of his men looked uneasy about staying in the vicinity any further. But at least the fighting off in the distance had stopped. He had thought of sending men in their direction to help them out, but splitting his forces wasn't wise, especially since he had Mirabella with him and that's what Vladek wanted more than anything else.

"You won't fight me any longer?" Leogane asked as Erlin ordered the men to build campfires and start a meal.

"Nay."

Leogane smiled a little. "You only say so because you believe your brother will take you beyond my reach."

"Would you even want me if you learn what I've said is true? That Inari isn't my uncle? That you will get nothing from this union but grief?" she asked.

She was right. And that was another reason for him wanting to remain here. He needed to know the truth.

"They are without horses," Mirabella said under her breath.

"What?"

She looked up at Leogane with tears in her eyes. "They've been trying to catch up to us on foot. No, wait." She held up her hand and then cast him a brilliant smile, chasing away the fear in her expression, warming her appearance by leaps and bounds. She truly was beautiful when he saw her this way. "They...they have managed to capture the dead knight's horses. They are riding toward us now."

"How do you know this?" He wasn't sure he could handle being married to a woman who possessed unusual powers, though she had aided them in battle with her gift and had been welcome.

"I hear them. Do you not hear the horses' hooves pounding on the earth?"

"Nay, and it could be the dark knights coming to battle us again."

"Nay, 'tis not. I heard one of his...um, warriors say to grab the dead knights' horses. I'm sure it is my brother and his party coming to meet up with us."

Leogane wished he could be as sure as she seemed. He glanced at Justina who was wringing her hands nearby. "Your maid said you have done some awful things to the servants and the like."

"I've only seen her twice and I've always been locked in the tower. What awful things has she said about me? I could do naught in the tower."

"I suspect she has lied for whatever purpose." Leogane had been suspicious of the woman from the very beginning. If Inari had treated the princess ill, then anyone on his staff could have felt justified in treating her with the same disrespect.

"I had thought to befriend her because I had no friends at the castle, but that will not be happening now."

"She will not go with us," Leogane said. He would not protect a person who attempted to sabotage his mission. He wondered then if she worked for Inari or if she was like the witch in the healer's hut, working with Vladek.

10

Argon was glad they finally all had horses to ride now. They would make much better time now and he thought they had to be drawing closer to Leogane and his men—if they didn't have to keep stopping to fight the dark knights. He swore Vladek's men were trying to keep him from reaching his sister. Then he thought he smelled smoke from campfires.

"Leogane has set up camp and they are preparing a meal," Talamaya said, confirming what he'd thought—or at least had hoped for.

Some of Vladek's men could have been setting up the campfires, so Argon was glad Talamaya could see it was Leogane and his men instead. Argon wished she was on his staff. Her future visions were most welcome. "Do you see us arriving at their camp before they leave? A fight between us ensuing? A peaceful meeting of forces?"

Talamaya shook her head as she rode in the lead, Gallant on a horse beside her. Argon had been amused that he had wanted to mount the fallen knight's horse out of Argon and the women's sight. Gallant was strong so Argon hadn't thought he'd have any trouble. After much cursing and demanding the beast hold still for him in the woods, he and the horse had finally joined them. Argon hadn't wanted him to leave the party like he had though. Gallant could have been attacked while out of their sight. But Argon realized Gallant didn't want to show he was having trouble mounting the tall dark knight's horse.

After trying to see anything further, Talamaya finally said, "I cannot see our arrival, but I can see that the duke has a fair amount of men. Appears to be—" She paused. "Not sure. Mayhap twenty or more? They move about and I only see partial frames of the setting. They are cooking a wild boar they managed to hunt."

"My sister, how does she appear to you?" Argon worried she might be tied up while forced to go with Leogane.

"Well. She's sitting on a log next to one of the fires, but she's peering into the woods in our direction, as if she can hear us. But we cannot hear them, so I doubt she can hear us."

Argon assumed Talamaya was correct, but he was glad his sister was all right. "And Leogane?"

"He was offering her a bite of spitted boar and she was accepting it. But she keeps watching in our direction like she knows you are coming for her."

Argon shouted, "I am coming, Mirabella!"

"Won't you warn them to move on?" Kersta asked. "If they think we are foe? Or they could even set up an ambush."

"I have to let her know I'm coming for her in the event she can hear me." Though Argon suspected Kersta was right. But he wanted to give his sister hope, if she could hear him, and let her know he was close by and coming for her.

"But she has not responded, so she must not be able to," Kersta said.

Talamaya said, "I see nothing else concerning the matter. But I see a tall ship battered by a storm."

"The Duchess?" Argon worried they'd be shipwrecked on this island forever.

"Another."

"Leogane's?" he asked.

"It flies a lion flag."

"Then Leogane's. But it doesn't mean my ship is not tossed about likewise." Then Argon frowned. "Do you see my sister aboard the ship?"

"I cannot see that."

"'Tis worse than frustrating," Gallant said.

"Would you rather Princess Talamaya not warn us of what is ahead, good or bad?" Kersta asked, sounding perturbed with the dwarf.

"Are ye daft, women? She has saved our bacon on several occasions with her future sight—good or bad." Gallant shook his head.

Kersta smiled and glanced down at the map spread out on her lap again.

Mexia said, "If you have not guessed it, the two of them are always like this with each other."

"I gathered as much," Argon said. "Are we still on the right path?" he asked Kersta.

"Aye, we are."

"Did you read the dark knights' minds?" Argon suddenly wondered if Kersta could. Mayhap that would give them some insight into what or who they were.

"Now that I think of it, they were mindless. Like when you controlled the sailors' thoughts on your ship. These men were told to kill us, and that was it. They thought of nothing else. Like the men on your ship who did their chores, but they thought of nothing else," Kersta said.

"This is dark magic though," Mexia said. "The fact they turn into dust makes me think of the skeletons and the undead we had to dispense with in the cemetery that one time. It's like they're being spawned also by some dark forces."

"Vladek," Argon said. He had to eliminate the count the first chance he had.

11

W hen Argon and three women and a dwarf came into view riding dark knight horses, several extra horses following them, Mirabella was thrilled and raced to see her brother. She was elated to see he wasn't hurt.

Argon leaped down from his horse and hugged the breath from her. "I feared I would never find you."

"I was afraid you wouldn't either, but then I saw the Duchess anchored offshore from the tower where I was locked away and prayed you would make it to me safely. I was worried the guards at the castle wouldn't release me to go with you though." Mirabella gave him another warm hug.

Argon cast Leogane a dark look. "You couldn't wait until I arrived to speak with my sister—"

"Your sister didn't tell me you were on the island trying to reach her," Leogane said in just as gruff a voice.

"Come, eat with us," Mirabella said, glancing at the dark-haired women and the dwarf. "Where are your men?" she asked her brother. She really was surprised they wouldn't be here with him. They couldn't have made it this far without more of a fighting force.

"He only needed us," Gallant said, pressing his hammer against his chest as if saying he meant Argon only needed the dwarf and his hammer.

"This is Princess Talamaya," Argon said, introducing them. "And Ladies Kersta and Mexia. That's Gallant."

"Royalty?" Mirabella had never known of royal women who fought on quests unless in self-defense. Which she would have done herself if someone would have given her a weapon.

"No' me," Gallant said.

"Aye, we are. Your brother kidnapped us after we paid him for safe passage home to Inherian," Kersta said.

Mirabella gaped at her brother. "You didn't." She knew him to be the most righteous of men. She couldn't believe he'd do something so low.

"They've accomplished miraculous feats, Mirabella. Zane has taken control of the army and the rest of our ships. Halton only just managed to gather enough of our crew and aided our escape on the Duchess before Zane could stop us. My sailors are better fighters when on the ship than on the land. I needed the ladies and Gallant to help me rescue you."

"But three women and a—"

"Guild adventurer and warrior," Gallant said. "Ye should have seen all the battles we've been in. From fighting the undead, dark elves, to answering the sphinx's riddles, to battling cheetaurs and red devil wolves, and any other manner of dangerous creatures. Cyclops even. You name it. With just the four of us." The dwarf pointed his war hammer at Argon. "He was not there."

"Cyclops?" Mirabella didn't believe anyone could fight them.

"We outwitted them." Gallant dismounted and Argon helped Kersta from her horse while Leogane went to Talamaya's aid and Erlin helped Mexia down.

Kersta was studying Leogane, and Mirabella wondered if she

fancied the duke. But would Leogane be interested in another princess instead? Talamaya? She was beautiful. Or even Lady Mexia? But neither of the other women paid Leogane any mind. Just Kersta.

And what Mirabella thought was even stranger was the way her brother watched Kersta. He seemed perturbed she was focused on the duke.

"You have never met the soothsayer Modi, Mirabella, but she foretold that these guild members would be intertwined with my quest to free you from the castle." Argon took a seat with the others at the campfire to eat. "I'd learned of their conquests for months before I had a chance to convince them to come with me on this quest."

"I am Leogane of Wendover," the duke finally offered, since no one had bothered to introduce him. "And this is my advisor, Lord Erlin."

"Whose daughter Lord Wendover wishes to wed," Mirabella said, annoyed.

Argon raised a brow. "If this is so, why did you take Mirabella from the castle?"

Leogane took a draft of his ale. "I spoke to this same soothsayer as you, it seems. She said naught about you or your traveling companions, but she said I needed to remove Princess Mirabella from the castle and take her from the island. That kingdoms were at stake or something cryptic like that. Is it true that your brother murdered your father?"

Appearing surprised at the news, Argon looked at Mirabella to see if she knew what Leogane was talking about.

"Aye, 'tis true, Argon. I witnessed it. Once you were gone with your envoy on the peacekeeping mission, Zane arranged the impromptu hunt. I wasn't supposed to be there, but I just felt something wasn't right. Zane was too eager to hunt with our father when he normally wanted to hunt with his friends instead and left you to hunt with him. Anyway, he didn't even have one of his men kill Father. He killed him himself and then said it was an accident."

"Did Zane see you witness our father's murder?" Argon asked, sounding concerned.

"I didn't think so. But he might have suspected it. He sent me off right after that. I was bound, blindfolded, and gagged in my chamber and removed at once. I had no idea where I was being taken. And then I was on a ship until I was taken to the island and then to the castle. On our journey to Leogane's ship, we came across a healer's hut. A woman there—who turned out to be one of these undead creatures or whatever they are, had killed the real healer and Leogane's men eliminated her. She said our mother was from Racine. Did you know that?"

Argon shook his head. "I didn't even think King Inari could be our uncle, but why else would Zane give you to him and then he'd pay a dowry to hand you off to some lord to form an alliance unless there was some truth to it?"

Leogane didn't seem to like where the conversation was leading and he said, "Eat up. We must leave at once. We only waited for your arrival. Whoever or whatever Vladek is, I'm sure we'll see more of him or his men before we can leave the island."

"My sister is not going with you," Argon said.

"Where is your ship anchored?" Leogane asked as they packed up the camp.

"On the other side of the island." Argon helped Kersta mount the dead dark knight's horse and the other men helped the rest of the ladies.

Mirabella couldn't believe her brother allowed Leogane to help her mount instead of doing it himself. And then to help Kersta? What was up with that?

"Then we'll take you there. You can't journey back across the island with your sister on your own. Vladek's men are after

Mirabella. If you take her with you, they will redouble their efforts to slip her away from you," Leogane said. "And you don't have much of a force."

"We made it here all in one piece, didn't we?" Gallant asked. "Much like you and your men when we have much fewer numbers."

"True," Leogane said, his voice tinged with admiration.

"Aye, we will go with you, Leogane," Mirabella said, before her brother could decline the offer. "I don't want to be on the island any longer. We're closer to Leogane's ship and even though you managed to get here on your own safely enough, I don't want to venture that way again with fewer numbers."

"There's a problem," Talamaya said. "A storm is coming in from the west. It will no doubt wreak havoc with both your ships. We won't be able to make it to the transport boats in time. There are caves near the shore. We'll have to take refuge there until the storm subsides."

"And you know this how?" Leogane sounded skeptical.

"I have second sight," Talamaya said.

"Oh, thank the goddess," Mirabella said. "I can hear things beyond what anyone else can hear. I was afraid to mention it to anyone for fear people would think I was a witch."

"I'm a mage," Mexia said, "so you are in good company." Then she frowned. "Did you hear us coming? Your brother calling out that he was coming for you?"

"Oh, aye, but no one in Leogane's party heard you. A mage. We have not had one working for our princedom. Mayhap we could hire you to work for us," Mirabella said.

"I have other plans," Mexia said.

Kersta was frowning as she looked about at the knights who were mounting their horses. "Are all these men well-known to you?"

Leogane glanced around at his men and turned to face her. "Aye, why do you ask?"

Erlin interjected then. "Five are new, my lord. Some of our men were ill before we traveled here, and we hired five new knights to take their places."

"So they are not all well-known to you," Kersta said.

"Nay. Again, why do you ask?" Leogane asked her.

"I've heard treasonous talk about stealing the princess away from you as soon as they're able. One accused another of killing their own men when they were supposed to be only pretending to do so," Kersta said.

"I would have heard them," Mirabella said.

Kersta shook her head. "Unless you have my gift, I doubt it."

"Call them forth," Leogane said to Erlin.

But when Erlin went to fetch them, the other knights warned him the men had taken off into the woods, saying they were going to check on something suspicious.

"Hopefully something else will eliminate them for us," Kersta said.

Argon looked surprised and Mirabella didn't understand how Kersta had heard the men speaking when she didn't since she was seated near her, and she could hear conversations from afar.

Argon finally said, "I can hide people's thought from others like the dark knights' thoughts were hidden from us."

"Since when?" Mirabella asked. Then she glanced at Kersta. "You can read minds?"

"Aye."

"Once I learned Kersta had her ability, I had to control the crewmembers' thoughts, or she would have known what I planned to do—take them hostage to assist me in saving you."

"I still can't believe you did that to these women."

"And me," Gallant said.

"So the knights weren't speaking out loud when you 'heard' them?" Mirabella asked Kersta.

"Nay. They were angry with each other, staying quiet lest someone loyal to Leogane overheard them. Then suddenly, their thoughts were silenced as if the men had died. Instead, I figure the one who was hiding their thoughts, like Argon can do, did that to them."

"Count Vladek," Mirabella said.

"He may have even been one of the men who had infiltrated your ranks," Kersta said.

"I want a description of these men," Leogane said to Erlin.

"Someone spoke to me through my thoughts. I can't read minds like Kersta, but he could speak to me in my head. I thought I was going mad," Mirabella said.

"This happened while you were in the hut with the witch? Why did you say naught about it?" Leogane asked, sounding irritated.

"I...I didn't know what to think. What if you thought I was crazy?" Mirabella frowned at the duke. "I've never had that happen to me before."

"If he can control minds and speak to someone telepathically, maybe I can too," Argon said.

"Try it," Mirabella said. "That could be useful."

Argon frowned with concentration and Kersta eyed him with speculation. "Did you hear me, Mirabella?" he finally asked.

"Nay."

"I did," Kersta said.

"But that's because you can read minds. I had hoped...I guess it's not to be." Argon sounded disappointed that his gift wasn't any more useful than that.

"What else did Modi tell you?" Talamaya asked Leogane.

When he wouldn't say, Kersta said, "He will find a wife on this quest."

"Who?" Mirabella asked.

Kersta shrugged. "Modi was cryptic like usual, but Leogane was able to decipher that much. If you're wondering, Princess Talamaya and Lady Mexia are already betrothed. So it wouldn't be about them."

Mirabella frowned at her, but then Erlin said, "Has anyone seen the maid who was supposed to be serving the princess?"

Talamaya said, "The yellow-haired lass? She left while everyone in camp was preparing the meal. She is with the dark knights and a man dressed as a mage, talking with him, like she was with him. I saw this in a vision."

"I knew it," Leogane said. "I knew there was something wrong with her."

"I thought so too," Mirabella said.

"Are you still thinking Vladek could be a possibility as far as a suitor goes?" Leogane asked Mirabella.

She shook her head. "He and his minions are evil. If he had his way, he wouldn't allow me to make a choice as to who I wanted to be with. There's no reason for him to fight you for my hand, and he's fought my brother too, intending to eliminate him as well. He's evil through and through."

"It's not your choice, Leogane, but mine," Argon said.

Mirabella scoffed. "Without King Inari's dowry, or an alliance with our own princedom, what use have I?"

They began to travel along the path through the woods to the beach and Leogane's ship, everyone keeping an eye out for further trouble, but at least she was glad her brother was with her and knew what she had seen Zane do to their father. She just hoped they could turn the tide against their evil brother.

"Once I have taken the princedom back, you will have a dowry and I will make a treaty with the man who would marry you, Mirabella." Argon couldn't help being annoyed with his sister. Once he took over rule of their people, he'd make sure she had someone to marry whom she was happy with and who would benefit their princedom. He would never force anyone on her, and he would ensure she was worth enough that she could find a suitable mate. "You will stay with one of the ladies until you can return home safely."

"We're from Damar," Talamaya said to Mirabella. "But after I see to business there, I'll be joining Lazarion as his queen."

"Ohmygoddess, the barbarian king?" Mirabella asked, sounding shocked and intrigued at the same time.

Argon was glad Lazarion hadn't offered for *his* sister's hand in marriage.

"Aye, the one and only."

"Or you can stay with me and with Prince Derek the mage I'm joining near the city of Langdon. We will be able to protect you sufficiently," Mexia said.

"You can stay with me in Damar. I can protect you there," Kersta said. "Not to mention the queen's forces would as well."

"I can fight," Mirabella said. "No one will give me a weapon so I can defend myself."

Kersta rode up next to her and unfastened her belt and handed her sheathed short sword to Mirabella. "Do not let these men get close to you, but should you have need, this will hopefully protect you."

"I don't think they'll try to kill me."

"It's not that. They'll want to grab you and take you to this Count Vladek. And then who knows if we would be able to get you back," Kersta said.

"You were reading Leogane's mind earlier when you were watching him so studiously, right?" Mirabella asked.

"Aye."

Leogane was riding to the right side of Mirabella and Kersta on her left so he could hear what was being said, though Argon wanted to hear what was going on also. He was riding behind Kersta, watching out for her. He was really fascinated by her, by what she could do with her abilities but also how loyal she was to her companions and even helping him with his quest. And though his sister seemed to have had some animosity for Kersta in the beginning, they seemed to be making some progress toward friendship. He was pleased Kersta had loaned his sister her short sword. He needed someone to look out for his sister when he couldn't, so he hoped Mirabella would stay with one of the ladies so she would be protected.

"I'll have to talk to you about what I learned later." Kersta gave Argon's sister a conspiratorial wink.

Concerning Leogane's thoughts? What was that all about?

"I'll help you in your quest," Leogane finally said, glancing back at Argon.

"With?"

"You have no army. I have one," Leogane said. "I also have ten ships at my disposal."

Argon was impressed. "I will take you up on it." He really didn't have a choice and he knew it would come with a price.

Mirabella gave Argon a look that said he better not think of making a deal with Leogane to hand her off to the duke to be his wife if Leogane helped him take back the princedom, unless she was agreeable.

But he wouldn't do that to Mirabella. The only way he would agree to their union was if both wanted it.

"Do not agree to take on this quest also," Gallant said to Talamaya.

"I will pay you more," Argon said, hoping to convince the companions to accompany them, using their special abilities.

They could really aid him, and from what Modi had said, he thought they were meant to help him further than just freeing his sister from the castle.

"Ye havena even paid for the first quest, finding and freeing your sister from the tower. And do no' say we didna help your sister escape confinement," Gallant said, "just because this duke got to her first."

Argon shook his head. He would be forever grateful to Gallant and the ladies' help. "Nay, you've helped me reach her when I would never have made it on my own. You've earned your pay. And you're helping to keep her safe until we can return her to the ship."

"So, woman?" Gallant asked Talamaya. "Aye or nay?" He studied her with narrowed eyes.

Talamaya sighed. "Aye. To right a wrong, we'll go with you, Argon."

"I'm all for it," Mexia said.

"It seems 'tis my destiny," Kersta said.

"Then I'm going also," Mirabella said.

Argon wanted to object. He wanted to keep his sister safe, but if those who would protect her best were staying with him, he had to keep Mirabella with him. What if Vladek continued to try and come after her even when Argon returned to his princedom? He feared he would until Argon could eliminate him.

"Ye will need me too then," Gallant said, sounding glad to be signing up for another quest, and not like he was being coerced into this. The dwarf was a mix of contradictions.

"When you made your way to the castle, did you have any trouble with these monsters?" Argon asked Leogane as the winds began to whip through the trees and he could barely hear anything other than the branches whipping about and the horses clip-clopping on the dirt path. Trees were bending in the harsh winds, and he feared they were dealing with a wind lash, not just a thunderstorm.

"No, nothing," Mirabella said.

Argon meant had Leogane and his men had any trouble! But he was glad Mirabella hadn't had any herself when she was first taken to the castle.

"Aye, we fought the dark knights several times on our journey to the castle," Leogane said. "I suspect they came after we did, before Count Vladek could take Mirabella from the castle. I'm certain he knew I was on a mission to fetch Mirabella. Though it sounds as though he and some of his men had been with us all along. Did you fight them earlier?"

"Aye, and we had a couple of centaurs with us who helped us and led us to the castle, but then they stayed there and would go no further," Argon said.

"The storm is upon us," Gallant said, as if they didn't already know it. "How much longer is it to the beach and the caves Princess Talamaya spoke of?"

"Not far," Leogane said. "We had no trouble on the beach at least."

Past tense. What if they did this time?

"But we dinna know what's in the caves," Gallant said.

Everyone glanced at Talamaya, who was pulling the hood of her cloak up over her head and securing it. "Do not look at me. I have no idea if we'll find trouble in the caves or even problems on the beach. All I know is that the caves could offer shelter when we desperately need it."

Just then, they heard a thunderous cracking noise and a tree of maybe a hundred feet tall snapped in half and everyone scattered as it toppled onto the path. Half of Leogane's men were on the side they needed to travel, along with Princess Talamaya, Erlin, and Mirabella.

Gallant, Leogane, Kersta, Mexia, and Argon with about

fifteen of Leogane's men couldn't move the horses over the fallen tree.

"Blasted," Gallant said, angry about being blocked from taking the route, but Argon knew he also didn't want to neglect his duty of protecting the princess.

Argon was just as aggravated and worried that his sister was on the other side of the massive tree, and he couldn't reach her quickly.

"Some of the extra dead dark knights' horses could still be with the princesses." Argon was ready to climb the downed tree to get to his sister.

"Wait. I can levitate you and your horse to the other side," Mexia said.

"It will take too long to do that with everyone," Leogane said. "In the meantime, our forces are divided."

It was not lost on Argon that Leogane included him and his party as part of the forces, when Leogane's men made up the bulk of them, and Argon appreciated the duke's comment.

"Right now, we have nearly half our forces on each side," Leogane said.

The rain poured down on them then in a deluge and the winds whipped around them with ferocity while they heard trees cracking in the forest all around them, before the giant, needled pines collapsed, knocking down others in their path.

"Go to the beach and the caves, Mirabella! We'll join you as soon as we can." Argon couldn't have his sister waiting for them to join her while the storm struck all around them with such fierceness.

"I can't levitate you against this wind," Mexia said, trying but it was of no use.

"We can climb over to see if any of the spare horses are still there," Argon said, but one of Leogane's men was already climbing to the top of the massive tree trunk about eight feet tall.

"One horse remains. Princess Mirabella has the horse in hand," the knight said.

"I'm going with them," Kersta said, jumping from her horse and trying to make the climb up the massive tree trunk.

Argon quickly dismounted and helped push her up so she could reach the top, the knight on top helping her the rest of the way. Argon wanted to go with her, but they needed to move quickly and if he didn't have a horse on the other side, he wouldn't be able to keep up in this storm. He'd slow them down, also, if he rode with someone. And he wasn't allowing anyone else to give up their horse.

"I'll help you down," one of Leogane's men told Kersta on the other side of the felled tree.

Once she disappeared from Argon's sight, she shouted, "I'm safe, on a horse, and heading out with the others!"

"Okay, so we go around the fallen tree as fast as we can," Argon said, worried that the other half of their party could run into more dark knights or other trouble. Not to mention the issue of what might be occupying the caves and they could need all of them there to help secure it. He wished Princess Talamaya was with them so she could tell them which was the best way to venture. If she could.

"Is the other party well on their way?" Leogane asked.

"Aye," his knight said. "Erlin got them on their way to shelter since both princesses were reluctant to leave until we joined them."

"Good. Can you see the shortest way around the fallen tree?" Leogane asked.

"Not for the forest. The tree was so tall, there's no telling," the knight said.

"To the right," Argon said. "There are fewer branches at the base of the pine trees. Fewer obstacles to navigate. And I believe this tree was closer to our path, so the top would be longer that way." He started to head to the right and Gallant and Mexia quickly joined him. Though the trunk would also be thicker this way.

Leogane directed his men to stick with them. The knight on top of the tree climbed down and mounted his horse, and they all followed Argon.

Argon had the notion they could split forces and half go each way so that at least half of the force on this side could find a faster way across and join and protect the princesses as soon as possible. As if Mexia knew what he was thinking, she said, "We cannot split our forces any more than they are right now. We need to stick together."

They were trying to pick their way through the thick under-brush against the harsh wind and rain, all of which was impeding their travel.

Kersta, I am meant to be yours, and you are meant to be mine. Argon hadn't been ready to think it out loud before, but he had to say it in his mind, wishing beyond anything that he would be able join up with Kersta on the other side sooner than later and she and his sister and the others would be all right. They just had to get beyond the tree trunk and then switchback to the path and catch up to the others.

But when they reached the base of the tree, they found they were at the edge of a raging river.

"Troll's dung," one of the knights said.

Now what? Their only options were to leave the horses behind and climb over the tree trunk or head the other way when they'd already wasted precious time going this way.

"Let's go the other way," Mexia said. "If we can get to where the tree trunk is narrower, we might be able to cut through some of it and make a path through the fallen tree. I can move parts of it with my talent once it's chopped away."

"Let's do it," Argon said, and he hurried to lead them back to the path and into the underbrush on the other side of the path, hoping to make up for lost time. Now he knew how Kersta had felt about taking the wrong trail earlier, though at least in her case, it had worked out to their benefit.

12

Despite the wind and rain and falling trees and who knew what else was out there, Kersta smiled at hearing Argon's unspoken thoughts before she was too far away from him. She wondered why he'd finally stopped trying to hide them from her.

Talamaya was riding beside her on the muddy path. "What makes you smile in the middle of all this chaos?"

"It seems Modi told Argon he and I are a match."

Talamaya looked sharply at her. "No."

"Aye. He's been trying to hide his thoughts about it all along."

"But you knew he was."

"Aye. You haven't seen anything about this?" Kersta asked, suspicious that her friend might have been keeping secrets from her also.

"Nay. You know I would have told you. And if I hadn't, you would have read my mind and learned of it." Talamaya smiled at her. "Are you happy?"

"To marry a prince who has lost his princedom, whose

brother wishes to murder him and has murdered his father, whose sister is—"

Mirabella glanced back at them. "Who is what?"

"You can hear us speaking?" Kersta asked, surprised.

"Oh, aye. It's remarkable. I might not be able to read minds, but I can hear like the hawk now," Mirabella said. "I told you that already."

"I'd forgotten you mentioned that. We ought to go together on quests," Kersta said.

Mirabella smiled. "Aye, I would like that." But then she frowned. "What is this about my brother and you?"

"You must have heard us and know what was said already."

"You are a match." Then Mirabella frowned again. "Wait, if you are a match with my brother and Leogane was supposed to find his mate on this journey—"

"There is only one other woman who is available that I know of," Talamaya said.

Mirabella looked straight ahead.

"If it is true, would you be agreeable?" Kersta asked, hoping it was. Often royals didn't find a match made in heaven, but one to fulfill an obligation to treaties and such.

"If Leogane helps Argon take over the princedom, I might be agreeable. He has no stake in helping us or in losing his men over such a fight unless he gains something from it. I doubt he wants only riches."

"Only if you wish it," Princess Talamaya said.

Mirabella cleared her throat. "I would be agreeable. Without his help, Argon couldn't manage taking over the princedom and our people will be at my brother Zane's mercy. Except for Leogane's interest in his advisor's daughter, I think we could suit."

"How does Erlin and his daughter feel about it?" Talamaya asked.

Talamaya was right. If Leogane's advisor and his daughter were upset with the situation, it could cause trouble for Leogane's rule, Kersta thought.

"His advisor and his advisor's daughter know what is best for his people," Erlin said, riding up beside Mirabella. "And for your information, no one else's, my daughter is in love with another man. We never speak of it because her duty is to Leogane, should he still wish to wed her, but if he chooses another, someone who is better for our people, then so much the better, aye?"

"I thought Leogane loved her," Mirabelle said.

"He thought so too, until he met you. You are what he needs while leading our people," Erlin said. "My daughter will be happy to serve you."

Kersta was glad for it. But she wished they hadn't been separated from the others.

"I hear growling," Mirabella said, "low in the underbrush beside the path."

"What is it?" Talamaya asked. "I can't see what it is. Can any of you?"

"Ogres!" cried a knight.

Not dark knights this time.

But this time, Talamaya brought out her scepter and swept it over the woods, and hideous screams pierced the air.

"What is that?" Mirabella asked, Kersta's short sword in her hand, ready to fight.

"The scepter of salvation that has magical powers of its own. But only Talamaya can wield it," Kersta said.

"You killed three of them with one blow," a knight said, sounding astounded.

"The others that were beyond your scepter's power are fleeing. The ogres are running back from whence they came," another knight said.

"The beach!" a knight said with excitement. "There's the beach!"

At least when they reached the beach, they didn't have to worry about the trees falling on them, but now the sand was blasting them in the high winds, and the waves crashed along the shoreline. They couldn't see any sign of the ship in the turbulent sea, the dark skies making it look like nighttime was upon them.

"To the caves," Erlin directed.

But Kersta wanted to wait for Argon and the others.

"Do not dally! To the caves," Erlin shouted again. "We may need your assistance in fighting who-knows-what in the caves."

Erlin was right. They didn't know what might have taken refuge in the caves and they would need all the help they could get to protect Princess Mirabella.

It was frustratingly slow going for Argon and his party as they backtracked to the path and then back into the woods through the thick underbrush. He hated making the wrong decision about the path to take. Everyone had relied on him to do the right thing and now Mirabella and the others were at risk because of that. Lightning flashed across the black clouds and thunder roared all about them still, the rain not letting up.

Trees were still falling, and the wind ripped branches off trees and sent them sailing through the air, hitting everyone in their path.

"Here," Mexia said, casting a spell, creating a bubble around them to protect them from the wind-driven branches. Then she moved to the heart of the tree and said, "Here, begin chopping the tree."

Several knights brought out axes and began chopping at the

tree while she continued to protect them from the storm. The rest watched for any signs of trouble.

Argon hoped the other party had made it to the beach already, away from the danger of the woods. Another tree cracked and everyone stopped to see where it would fall. It slammed into the woods some distance away, not far enough away for safety's sake, the impact shaking the ground and making several stumble. But then they were back to work, chopping at the tree in their way.

Mexia quit protecting them with the bubble and began levitating the cut branches and chopped wood and tossing them out of their path until they could begin the trek one horse and rider at a time through the carved-out path.

"Let's go," Argon said, and Leogane agreed, having some of his men go first to clear the path if they had trouble, the rest following behind as Mexia went next, Gallant following, Argon after that, and Leogane and the remainder of his men behind them.

Once they had all gathered on the other side of the tree, they hurried through the underbrush to reach the path again. Then they raced along the trail to try and reach the others at the beach as soon as they could. They saw no signs of bodies, which was good, and only horses' hoof prints in the mud.

Soaking wet, he was at least glad the island temperatures were warm so they weren't also chilled. Though once they were in the cave, they'd need to change into dry clothes and light a fire if they could.

"Dead bodies," one of the knights suddenly said.

Mexia looked at the ogres' lightly haired, green bodies. "They are burned with a single sword-like stroke. Princess Talamaya used the scepter on these three."

"A scepter did that?" Leogane said.

"The scepter of salvation."

Leogane's eyes widened. "You are the women—"

"And me," Gallant said.

"That went on the quest for the scepter and fought the wizard Grimoria."

"Aye, we did," Mexia said.

"No wonder you didn't need a force to come here to save your sister," Leogane said to Argon. "Are you sure you will need my forces to help you take back your princedom?"

"Aye. I don't want to kill my people who are under my brother's influence. They will work for me once I can eliminate him. There's only a small core of people he surrounds himself with that I need to destroy. Until I can reach them, I need all the help I can get."

They didn't find any more ogre bodies after that. If there were more ogres, they must have made themselves scarce. But then they found half a dozen dark knights' armor and tunics scattered on the ground.

It wasn't long after that sighting, that they saw the beach and he couldn't believe it had been so close to where the tree had fallen and stopped them.

Talamaya and the others were huddling close to each other beside the caves, the wind-driven sand and wind blasting them. Why weren't they inside the cave?

"Mexia, tame the dragons," Talamaya called out.

Mexia rode to the cave entrance and leapt off her horse. "How many?"

"Two. A male and a female. A couple. We haven't gotten close enough to speak with them. They don't want us to enter the cave," Talamaya said.

"These don't know the others we befriended?" Mexia asked.

"We are on the Emerald Isle of Mists, far from our continents where we befriended the dragons. I don't think they've met the others," Talamaya said. "You have a special ability with them. Tell them we only seek shelter until we can leave on the ship."

"You do too, princess," Mexia said before entering the cave and Argon joined her. She glanced at him. "You shouldn't be in here."

"We have dragons in our mountains. I speak dragon."

Kersta raised her brows.

"'Tis true. He can speak with them, but I've never learned how," Princess Mirabella said. "My fault, really."

"We come in peace," Argon said "From continents far from here. We've come to free my sister from the castle here and we're leaving on our ships as soon as the storm subsides."

The male dragon lowered his red, scaly head. The female raised her golden head. "You may enter but watch out for the eggs. I would prefer that you leave your weapons outside the cave but there are so many inhospitable creatures about, keep them. Before we allow all those knights and yourselves a place to stay, you must promise to do three tasks for us."

"Aye." Argon would do anything within reason, though he wanted everyone out of the storm and away from anything else that could harm them no matter what.

"What is it like on your continent?"

"If you mean to live as dragons, they love the mountains and caves they call their own. We allow no one to hunt them. Dragons are sacred to us. Many of us know dragon speak. My sister has neglected her studies though," Argon said.

Mirabella called into the cave, "I intend to rectify that at once."

"We don't know if we'll be accepted there, but this island is too inhospitable for our offspring. We've already had trouble with several ogres. We can manage, but dragonlings cannot," the female said. "We would have you take us with you and speak on our behalf to the dragons who live there. Not all are accepting of foreign dragons. Our own island had an active volcano and it finally erupted, and the island is now uninhabitable. If you didn't know, this island also has an active volcano and we wouldn't wish to face the same situation as before, especially with young dragonlings, or even before they're hatched."

"Okay, so we take you on our ship, but we have a problem," Argon said.

"You need to oust your brother from power, so we overheard your sister saying to the other princess." The male sighed.

"We were going to take Princess Mirabella to Inherian to keep her safe. You can stay there until we can move you to Argon's princedom. Or you can stay with the mages where I'll be moving to," Mexia said. "In other words, we will take you somewhere safe until you decide where you'd like to settle."

"You are friends of the dragons," the female said.

"Aye."

"You said you required us to make three promises. What else would you have us do?" Argon wanted to get everyone moved into the caves as quickly as possible.

"Ren needs a tooth pulled. It's infected and he's cranky most of the time. Pull it and that will be your second requirement," the female said.

"Can I see it?" Mexia asked.

Argon wasn't sure how he was going to remove the dragon's tooth without putting him in a lot of pain and getting incinerated for it, but he sure didn't want Mexia to be responsible for it.

When he put his hand on her shoulder to stop her, she smiled at him. "I'm a healer. If I can heal the infection with my healing pack and magic and save the tooth—"

"Even better," the female said.

"Open wide," Mexia said, drawing close to the dragon's huge head and wicked teeth. "Oh." She wrinkled her nose.

"Bad breath, I know. That's because of the infection," the female said.

Argon drew closer to help Mexia. "Oh, there. It's a splinter of a bone stuck in the gum."

"I told him so. But I didn't have any way to remove it." The female watched them closely. "He kept insisting his tooth needed to go."

Even though it was a splinter, it was large, and Argon grabbed hold and pulled, but he couldn't get it out it was so slippery.

Leogane joined them and between the two of them, he and Argon yanked and pulled until they felt it give and out came the shark bone that had been wedged into the gum, Argon still holding onto it. They both fell on their backsides.

"Okay, now I'm going to apply some healing ointment and then use some of my healing abilities to speed up the process." Mexia began to work on the infection, adding the ointment, drawing out the infection, and starting the healing process. "It will take a few days and then it should be well on the mend. He might need to stay away from bones for a few days."

"And the third quest?" Argon asked.

"Tell your people to come in out of the storm," she said, her mate resting his head on the eggs as if he were worn out from the tooth issue.

Leogane told everyone to come in and get out of the bad weather.

"Okay, for the third request, we'll need a nest egg to get us started. We had to abandon our mountain of gold that is now melted and under layers of molten rock," she said.

"Wait, we haven't been paid yet for our services," Gallant said. "Ye cannot promise the dragons any more gold that you do not have."

"I have gold and since more of those who are here are

beholden to you are *my* people, I will pay what you need," Leogane said. "As to the ship to take you to someplace safe, I can also do this. It will be your choice as to where you wish to reside. It sounds to me like you have several options available to you."

"Thank you for helping my poor mate out. This is the first time he has been able to sleep in days now," the female said. "And we'll decide where we want to go once we have seen for ourselves which location suits us best."

Everyone began pulling spare clothes out of packs and the women went deeper into the cave to change into dry things while the men dressed near the dragons.

"You can speak our language also," the female said to Leogane.

"Aye. Like where Argon resides, we are friendly with our dragons, and no one is allowed to hunt them. We don't have any of your coloring. They are brown, or green. I know for a fact they go in search of dragons from afar to bring knew genes into the flock of dragons. As for your clutch of dragon eggs, our dragons love dragonlings, so they will be welcome," Leogane said.

Mexia laughed in the back of the cavern. "Tell me it isn't true."

Argon wondered what that was all about.

"Aye. 'Tis true," Talamaya said.

"Hmm, so none of us might be returning to Damar for good then. Except to visit with our families from time to time." Mexia sounded amused. "And to think no one thought we could survive outside our kingdom before we went on our first quest and returned with the scepter of salvation."

13

"Well, go to him," Talamaya said. "You need to prove to yourself that Argon is the one for you."

Mexia shook her head. "I'm still drying Kersta's hair." She was using a spell of heat and air that rippled through the strands of hair and felt heavenly against Kersta's scalp.

Otherwise, Kersta, though in dry clothes now, still felt chilled in the chilly cave because her hair was wet. Kersta scoffed. "He has been fighting letting me know the truth. Is it because he hasn't wanted it to be true?"

"He has been in denial that it could be true," Mexia said.

"Why are you taking care of my hair first?" Kersta asked, thinking by rank, Mexia should have dried Princess Talamaya's hair first, then Princess Mirabella.

"Because you have business to take care of that requires a personal touch." Mexia raised the heat level on Kersta's hair, and her hair was finally dry.

"Well, go to him," Mirabella prompted as she began braiding Kersta's hair while Mexia worked on drying Talamaya's hair. "Talamaya is right. Though I can tell you he is loyal and kind when it comes to our people. Father sent him to make peace with another realm because he can keep his temper under pressure, unlike our brother Zane."

"What about the negatives?" Kersta asked.

"Oh, that." Mirabella smiled rather devilishly. "He is rather fond of his sword, above all else. He sleeps with it night and day."

"Which is understandable," Kersta said, "if others should wish him harm."

"Aye, of course. He can be evasive if he doesn't want you to know his thoughts on a matter, or his feelings."

Which Kersta had already learned.

"You know, he might not have revealed the truth to you in his thoughts because he wasn't sure of them himself," Mirabella said. "Or was in denial."

"Aye, that could be."

"He can be rather cynical."

"Oh, I imagine. It is easy when you believe in people and find they betray you."

"Aye, you too then?" Mirabella asked.

Kersta smiled. "A time or two. He can also be...deceitful—for a cause."

"Because he took you hostage and drugged you and your companions? I had not thought he had it in him. He is usually very honest, but I'm sure it all had to do with feeling he had no other choice. He couldn't pay for an army to come free me. And he couldn't do it without help. He went to Modi to learn how he could save me and the four of you were our salvation." Mirabella finished braiding Kersta's hair.

Kersta thanked her and was going to braid Talamaya's while Mexia moved to dry Mirabella's.

"Go, Kersta. Quit putting this off." Talamaya smiled. "Mirabella will braid my hair."

Kersta frowned. "All right, all right. But it doesn't mean he will be any more forthcoming now than he was earlier." Except she smiled. He had said he was hers as she was his—in his thoughts before she'd rode out of earshot—or beyond her ability to listen into his thoughts. She realized she'd been trying to listen to them often when they were together, curious as to what he was thinking—mostly about her. But he'd worked hard to keep his thoughts hidden, filling them with the sights and sounds surrounding them instead.

Sure, he had been concerned about the beasts that might attack them, but he'd also been purposefully hiding his thoughts from her, she felt.

She moved closer to the front of the cave where the men had started a campfire, the smoke vented out through a natural vent in the rock. Stalactites holding tight to the ceiling reached down like daggers toward the floor some twenty feet above them. Columns made from the dripping minerals had formed in various locations like structures built to hold up the cave's ceiling.

She heard chittering way up above and figured a few bats were living up at the top of the cave.

The female dragon had lain her head on top of her eggs in a protective manner.

Leogane was sitting with Argon, looking out at the pouring rain, the trees still snapping in the woods beyond the beach.

She read Argon's thoughts now—his worry about the men on his ship, the ship itself. She appreciated that he cared about his people so dearly.

He took a deep settling breath.

Leogane was feeling the same way. Concerned about the sailors, his ship, and even Argon's own people. He was thinking about Mirabella—about how he'd thought her so unsuitable until he'd traveled with her for some time and realized she wasn't at all like what he had thought. She was gentle, but she was willing to fight against their enemies, not afraid for herself, but afraid for everyone else.

Kersta raised a brow. Why wasn't Argon thinking about her? About Kersta?

And then he turned to see her standing there next to the campfire where others had gathered, staying warm. He smiled with such a warm smile, she felt heat fill her all the way through.

Then he lost the smile and hurried to rise and join her. "What is wrong?"

"You are the one who..." She glanced at Leogane's men and Gallant listening to see what she had to say. She didn't want to say what she had to in front of everyone else.

"Who?"

"Forget it. We'll talk when we don't have an audience." Kersta couldn't help sounding annoyed. Once she wanted to get something off her chest, she did it.

But then her friends came to her rescue.

"Go," Princess Talamaya said. "We'll visit with the others while the two of you can speak in private in the back of the cave."

Kersta took Argon's hand and led him back to where the ladies had been and instead of talking, she wrapped her arms around his neck and kissed him.

ARGON COULDN'T BELIEVE Kersta was kissing him, but he wasn't missing the opportunity to kiss her right back. He cupped her face and kissed her with as much ardor as she was kissing him. And then she pulled her mouth away from his and raised her brows.

"You didn't have to hide that you are the one for me."

He chuckled. "I wasn't sure if you...or I...was ready to deal with it."

"Considering we had to save your sister, aye." Then Kersta frowned at him. "You are not hiding anything about your sister from me, are you?"

He sighed. "Nay, except that she would find the man she was meant to be with. I have no idea if it is Leogane or someone else."

"But the prediction he received was that he would find the woman of his dreams here and there's only one other woman that could mean."

"You are taken."

Kersta laughed. "Aye. I have chosen you. But what of the woman who had accompanied your sister?"

"She is gone. Besides, I don't believe the duke would offer to help us with his forces if he hadn't decided he wanted to offer for my sister. What about us?"

"You would have to ask my parents for my hand in marriage. They might not agree that you would be good enough for me if you have no princedom to call your own."

He smiled at her. "I will regain my princedom and you will rule beside me. Will that sway your parents to approve of me?"

"Mayhap. My other suitors will not be happy."

Again, Argon smiled. "If they are your suitors, why have they allowed you to fend for yourself with your lady companions and a dwarf, endangering yourself all the while? Why would they not be accompanying you on your quests? They are not worthy of your hand."

Kersta had to agree with Argon there. "Ahh, but you believe you are worthy when you had taken me—and my companions —hostage to free your sister."

"For a goodly sum."

"That you do not own, as Gallant loves to mention."

"You will gain a sister. You won Mirabella over when you entrusted her with your sword."

"She says you sleep with your trusty sword."

"Always. I know you sleep with your deadly staff."

"Always. We make a pair." She smiled at him.

"I wholeheartedly agree."

She wanted to see his princedom first, his people. What if he —and his sister seemed agreeable—were the only ones who wished her to be his wife? They might not like that a baron's daughter from the Kingdom of Damar would be the prince's choice of a wife. Not just because she wasn't a known quantity, but also because she would help him to rule.

"If you take your princedom back, will I help you to rule it?"

"I would want it no other way. My mother ruled beside my father in all ways."

"Oh, then I agree."

He chuckled.

"It hasn't been that way in Damar," she explained, "though things have changed since Talamaya retrieved the scepter and her mother now rules the kingdom after Talamaya's father died."

"Aye, well, if I'm off fighting—and you're not with me to help me battle our foes—then you will be managing our realm, making sure no one else tries to take it over while I'm away. We cannot have a repeat of what my brother pulled."

"That works for me."

Kersta couldn't believe how much her life had changed since going with Talamaya and Mexia on the princess's first quest. She couldn't believe that all three of them had found mates beyond the Kingdom of Damar. Though they still had much to do before that could happen, she was saddened too, to think their quests would end. That they would settle down and live lives with their mates and only tell their own children someday of the great feats they had accomplished—of the rugged terrain they had crossed, the beasts and humans they had fought, the puzzles they'd solved—all to right so many wrongs.

"What...what if I had to go on a quest from time to time?"

He smiled. "You would have to be a member of the adventurer's guild in Miramar."

Her lips parted in surprise. "Could I?"

"Aye, with my strongest recommendation for approval. You and your companions have done more than any adventurer I've ever hired to accomplish some mission has done. You are already a member of the adventurer's guild for the whole of the continent of Albion. But I would hope you would have companions with you who are just as good at achieving the quests as the ones you travel with now."

"I probably could entice Gallant to come on one...or two. The others might be too busy." But Kersta would not feel right about undertaking a guild quest without all her companions there at hand. They worked too well as a team.

"I'm certain you will have only but to ask. But first, we must take on the perilous journey to free my people from my brother's rule."

"The rain is letting up," Talamaya called out. "The storm is subsiding."

But it wasn't. It was still coming down hard. For a few minutes more. Then suddenly, it slowed to a trickle and for the first time since they'd taken shelter in the cave, they saw the sun's rays poking into the entrance.

"The winds have blown the mist away. Hurry. We must get to the ship and navigate to yours before the mist envelopes the island again," Leogane said, rushing out of the cave, his sword in hand as if he expected to fight monsters on the beach.

There was nothing there but the sand and the surf, transport boats being launched, and at least Leogane's ship was still bobbing up and down on the churned-up sea.

"We can fly some of you out to the ship so it won't take as long," the female dragon said. "But you must carry our eggs. We can, but one only each at a time. Take care and do not drop them or crack them."

"We'll take you up on it," Leogane said, pacing across the beach, intermittently looking back at the woods, expecting trouble, or out to the sea, waiting for his men to get there.

"Carry my eggs to the beach now," the female dragon said.

The eggs were large, but lightweight, and each of the men grabbed an egg and hurried them to the shore, settling them gently on the wet, white sand so as not to crack them. They saw the transport boats coming—three of them, large enough to take twenty to thirty horses at a time. Once they reached the shore, the sailors looked surprised to see the dragons and the eggs.

"We carry the eggs with us. The dragons will fly some of us with them so we have enough room for the extra cargo," Leogane said.

The horses were walked up a ramp onto the first of the boats, which were divided into three horses per stall, each supported by a sling. In the section where the sailors had spare canvas sails and blankets, the men hurried to set the eggs so they wouldn't roll around and crack on the journey across the rolling sea.

"I will go with the first transport ship," Kersta said, not wanting to ride a dragon.

"I will stay with you then," Argon said.

She smiled at him. "You had your heart set on riding a dragon. You have never done so."

"You read my mind." He sighed.

"Aye. Go ride a dragon."

"Nay. If something happens to the transport, I want to be here with you."

Now that was the kind of chivalrous thing she'd want to hear from a prospective mate. The sailors began rowing the boat as Mexia, Gallant, and Talamaya rode the female dragon, and Leogane and Mirabella—who Kersta thought was starting to believe the duke was right for her—rode the male dragon.

The rest of the men and the remainder of the horses were divided among the last two boats and soon followed after the first of the transports.

The sea tossed the boat around and Kersta wondered if she should have ridden a dragon instead.

Argon wrapped his arms around her and sat with her next to the eggs on the canvas nest. "Do you feel the same as me?"

"About riding the dragon?"

He smiled. "Aye."

She chuckled. "Sometimes I make the wrong choices."

"We are all fallible."

Then Kersta heard a woman shouting from the beach and she and Argon stood to see who it was. "The woman who had accompanied your sister and then disappeared from the camp."

"Wait for me! Don't leave me!" Justina shouted.

"Should we go back for her?" one of the sailors asked Argon, though the prince was not in charge of Leogane's men.

But maybe they figured he was a man of import and knew something of the situation since he had been traveling with Leogane.

Before he could respond to the man's question, Kersta said, "Nay, we do not go back for her. She works for the dark knights, for Vladek."

The sailor who had asked the question looked to Argon for guidance.

"I read her mind. If we were to return and land on the shore to pick her up, the dark knights would attack. They are awaiting our return, standing in the shadows of the woods. Do not go back to the shore," Kersta said.

"Do as the lady says. Continue rowing to the ship," Argon said.

Then they heard a roar on the beach and saw dark knights racing across the beach, some with bows and arrows aimed to shoot at them, but all the boats were beyond their reach now. Their ploy hadn't worked.

"Your gift is great," Argon said.

"I sometimes feel it's not enough. Not as grand an ability as Mexia's mage talents or Talamaya's gift of foresight. I can only read minds, and not of monsters', just human and elves, dwarves, and other creatures who have like minds. Look how I couldn't even read yours and learn what you were up to with regard to me and the rest of my companions."

"Aye, but you shouldn't regret it." He took her into his arms and sat her down next to him and they snuggled. "We might have been taken in by the woman if we hadn't learned what she was thinking."

"I wonder why Vladek didn't hide her thoughts from me, like he did the dark knights." Kersta wished she'd had more time to listen to the woman's thoughts earlier.

"Maybe he has conjured up the dark knights, but he has persuaded the woman to work for him and she's not the same as them."

"And the witch at the healer's hut? She died in the same manner as the dark knights."

"I suspect she was one of their kind. Do not ever regret that your gift isn't that great, Kersta. Though I feel that way about mine sometimes."

"That you can control what people are thinking about?"

"Aye." Argon shrugged. "What good does it do if I can do this feat unless it's to protect them from you using your ability on them? And that's only when I know someone has your talent that's around at the time."

She smiled. "To keep me from learning all your dark secrets should they know them."

He laughed. "They better not think of anything but all the good I do."

"Oh, I am so looking forward to seeing if that is so."

Argon smiled.

She truly cared for him. Instead of making her feel inadequate, he had turned this around so that she was excited about learning all there was to know about him.

"Mama," she heard something say.

She glanced down at the eggs. "Ohmigoddess, one of the dragonlings is looking for her momma." She ran her hand over the egg. "We are taking you to your momma and your father on the boat to the ship and sailing away to a place where you and your brothers and sisters can live in peace with your parents." She had heard they were like chickens communicating from within the eggshell while the hen clucked back at them until they were hatched.

A small pecking sound started at the top of the bluespeckled shell.

"Oh, no, no, no, you must wait to rejoin your mother and father on the ship first," she warned, the ship rolling on the stormy seas, the sun hiding behind new clouds, the sky darkening, yet rays of sunlight still poked through. She was afraid of what the dragon mother had said—don't crack the shells. But there was no stopping the little dragonling who was trying to make her way out of the shell.

Another crack.

"What do we do?" Kersta asked, feeling panicked. She knew some species became attached to the first object they saw when they came out of their eggshells—imprinting, and she was afraid that's why the mother was worried about cracking the shells prematurely if the mother or father wasn't there for the dragonlings to imprint on.

"Row faster!" Argon called out. "The dragonlings are hatching. We must reach the ship so they can rejoin their parents before the dragonlings emerge from their shells."

That was enough incentive for the sailors to put their backs into it, despite the rough seas they had to navigate.

Kersta just hoped it would be enough.

14

Mirabella heard the dragonlings calling out to their mother and father and she glanced back to see the boat moving through the rough seas, but the little ones were ready to break free from their shells. "One of the dragonlings wants out of its shell," she shouted to the father.

He glanced over at his mate.

"I will return for her," the female dragon said. She turned around and with her mighty wings, she flew back to the transport boat.

Then she hovered over the boat for a moment. "I'm afraid to set down. That I'll swamp the boat. But I must be with my little ones when they emerge from their shells."

"Only one dragonling is trying to make its way out of the shell," Kersta said to the mother.

"All right. I will take her." The dragon swooped down and grabbed the partially cracked egg in her mouth, then flew back toward the tall ship.

Then the male dragon landed on the deck of Leogane's ship and Mirabella was glad that Leogane was with them because his sailors gasped and looked affright to see the dragons landing on the ship. Mirabella and Leogane quickly slid off the back of the dragon and landed on the deck. Then the female joined them with the cracked shell in her mouth, a small dragonling's head poking out.

Kersta called out, "Another shell is cracking!"

The female dragon set the dragonling in its cracked shell on the deck, while Talamaya, Gallant, and Mexia dismounted.

"Another dragonling is trying to break out of its shell," Mirabella said to the female.

"The next one is yours," the female said to her mate, and he immediately lifted his wings and flew off to retrieve the dragonling. The female spoke to her newly hatched dragonling. "You are coming early, little one."

And then the dragonling was out of her shell, snuggling with her mother. Mirabella and everyone looked on at the sight with awe and joy. In all the darkness that they'd encountered, seeing the baby inspired them to continue to help others in need.

Mirabella had never thought of herself as someone who would take on quests, but Talamaya and her companions had also inspired her to do what she had never thought possible.

She'd even managed to use Kersta's sword to strike at a couple of the dark knights who had attempted to grab her on the journey during the last attack before they reached the shore. She'd only fought in practice sessions for defensive purposes back home, so she was glad Kersta had loaned her the sword and she was successfully able to deter the knights.

The father dragon brought back the half-cracked egg and set it next to the mother as the dragonling finished breaking out of its shell.

By then, the boat was being pulled up, the horses offloaded onto the tall ship, and the men hurried to carry the dragon eggs to the mother where she was protectively curled around her first two hatched dragonlings before any more dragonlings hatched.

Even Argon and Kersta were carrying an egg each to bring to the mother in a hurry, both of the shells cracking as the dragonlings tried to peck their way out of their eggs. It was as if they had heard the others were free and wanted to be free too.

Mirabella went to get one, but Leogane caught her hand. "They've got this. You can go to the captain's quarters and you and the others will be served a meal. I'll join you soon."

"What about sailing to meet up with Argon's ship?"

"Aye, as soon as all the transport boats have returned, we'll make our way to the Duchess." Leogane saw the last transport boat secured. He gave orders for them to sail around the coast until they reached the Duchess. "But hurry. The fog is beginning to enfold the island in mists again."

They put up the sails and caught the wind and headed for the Duchess as Mirabella, Mexia, Gallant, and Talamaya were escorted to the captain's quarters.

ARGON WAS RELIEVED they were sailing to his ship and that Leogane was good for his word. He was also grateful that none of the hatching dragonlings had imprinted on him or Kersta. He held her hand and brought her over to where she could see his ship off in the distance.

"It looks intact," she said, her voice full of relief.

"Aye." He had worried that with all the troubles he'd had thus far, that his ship might have sunk to the bottom of the sea during the storm. He was also anxious that his men would believe Leogane's ship was there to fight them. "I need to get word to them that we're friend, not foe," Argon said to Kersta.

Leogane came up behind him and slapped him on the back. "Food and ale are being served in the captain's quarters. It will be over an hour before we reach your ship and then we'll use the horn to speak to your crew."

"Aye. Thank you." Argon took Kersta's hand. "We'll eat now."

"Did any of the dragonlings imprint on you?" Leogane asked, sounding amused.

"Nay, lucky for us," Argon said. "I'm not sure how the mother would have felt about that."

Then they went into the captain's quarters, and all sat down to eat fish stew and drink honeyed mead or ale.

"We worried about you and the dragonlings," Talamaya said, reaching out to take Kersta's hand and squeezed it.

"Aye, no more than us!" Kersta squeezed the princess's hand back, then released hers, picked up a piece of smoked cheese, and took a bite of it.

Gallant waved his bread at her. "Can you imagine having a dragonling to take care of on our adventures?"

"Nay," Kersta said. "We have problems enough as it is."

Mexia smiled. "I think you would make a good companion for a dragonling."

"Ha! You are the dragons' friend," Kersta said.

"So are you, and Talamaya," Mexia said.

"And me," Gallant said.

They all chuckled about that.

"When we reach my ship, will you go with me?" Argon asked Mirabella. He didn't want to take it for granted that she wanted to be with him on the ship, if she was getting to know Leogane.

The duke looked at her to see her response. She seemed indecisive. Then she smiled broadly. "I'll be with you on the Duchess, brother. I need to know more about Kersta and her companions and their adventures. And I need our sailors to know that you rescued me from the island. It will bolster them when we have to free the princedom from our diabolical brother."

Leogane looked disappointed and Argon understood how he felt. He would have felt the same way if Kersta, he realized, had said she wanted to stay with Leogane's ship and not travel with him.

"Aye, a good plan," Leogane said, "to help forge our friendship."

The companions all smiled at him, looking pleased he had been so gracious and hadn't tried to change Mirabella's mind.

When they were finally closer to the ship, Argon was up top, calling out on the horn to his men. "Prince Argon here with his sister and Prince Talamaya and her companions. We're returning to the ship now."

His crew cheered at the news. Argon knew they were ready to get on their way.

Everyone who was returning to the Duchess loaded onto a transport boat to be lowered into the rough sea and rowed to the Duchess in a hurry, the mist already cloaking the island and beginning to spread out in their direction.

Once they were received on the deck, the sailors cheered again.

Argon glanced up to see a dark shadow over them and saw the male dragon swooping over them and then down into the sea, fishing for their new little ones and the momma, probably. Sure enough, he came up out of the sea, water pouring off him, a school of marlins in his beak-like mouth. Then he dropped back onto Leogane's ship and shared the fish with them. But he quickly rose back up into the sky and Argon thought he was going on another fishing expedition. Instead, he swooped down onto the Duchess and deposited more of the marlins for his own men to eat.

"Thank you," Argon said, inclining his head to the dragon.

"We had plenty for ourselves and much more to share in that catch," the dragon said, then flew off the deck and returned to

Leogane's ship where the dragons and dragonlings were having a feast.

"Prepare the fish for the men," Argon said to his cook, and several of the sailors helped carry the fresh marlin to the kitchen. They hadn't eaten any fresh food in ages and he knew his men would enjoy a feast as they began to get the ship underway.

The bos'n mate slapped Argon on the shoulder. "We weren't sure you would ever return. And to free your sister and gain an ally? Good work, my lord."

"The duke wants to wed Mirabella."

Halton frowned. "Would you be agreeable?"

"'Tis up to my sister," he said as his sister and the other women retired with Gallant to the captain's quarters. "The duke promises to aid us in taking over the princedom with an army and ships."

"Then she must marry the duke."

Argon ran his hands through his tangled hair. "If she wishes it. And he does."

"I hope she wishes it then. And that he does."

"Aye." Argon hoped so too. For the first time, he had reason to believe he would be able to win this battle with his brother and that his sister could be happy with a good prospect for a mate.

Kersta came out of the captain's quarters to join him. "The male dragon said for giving his family a home, he would fight on our behalf."

"But he has a family he needs to protect," Argon said.

"Aye, but he said this is what he and his mate wish to do for us for taking them from the island and offering them so many safe choices of places to live and taking care of the shark bone in his gum too."

Argon wrapped his arm around her shoulders and pulled

her close. "Will you protect my sister when we go into battle?"

"Aye, I will."

And then he kissed Kersta in front of his crew. He swore his men all ceased speaking and turned to watch him. He might have known she would be his princess, but no one else had a clue and he'd wanted to keep it that way. Until now.

She would be at risk helping to fight his battles and protect his sister. He wanted his people to know what she meant to him.

She kissed him back and hugged him tight. "We will win this war."

He knew it to be true, only because she and her companions would be with him in the fight. "We will have to draw on the duke's forces before we can fight my brother."

Kersta frowned.

"What's wrong?"

"I hear"—Kersta quit speaking and pointed to three ships headed for them—"Prince Derek to the rescue."

"Prince Derek? Mexia's betrothed?" Argon asked, surprised, concerned that word had somehow reached the mage that he'd taken Mexia hostage.

Mexia was up on deck right after that, waving her hands in a way that meant she was casting a spell or sending communication to the prince, Argon suspected.

"Those are Derek's ships. Has he come to rescue you?" Kersta asked, joining her friend and Argon went too, wanting to assure the mage that Mexia was working with him, and that she wasn't his hostage!

"Ever since we did not return to the kingdom of Damar on time, he and King Lazarion were duly informed. Apparently, the king is on his way as well," Mexia said.

Coming to meet up with them, Talamaya smiled. "He is indeed. Are you able to message him in a mage way?"

"Nay, but I'm able to speak with Derek and he can send a

message to the king. King Lazarion's ships are not far behind Derek's ships. Derek doesn't know what Lazarion will do, but the prince vows to offer his knights and some of his mage friends who came with him to help in the battle ahead. Your brother doesn't know the power you shall wield," Mexia told Argon.

"I'm afraid I have only my own services to offer ye, Prince Argon," Gallant said to him, joining the companions.

"And that is good enough." Argon couldn't have been more thrilled to have all these allies, though it was only because of the ladies that it had happened. And only, he suspected, because he had taken them hostage. Their betrotheds had united to come and rescue them.

Mirabella joined them too. "Seems your taking the ladies hostage—"

"And me," Gallant said, folding his arms.

"Brought the forces together." Mirabella smiled at Gallant.

"Aye." But Argon figured they would have words with him about his highhandedness in doing so. He figured the men would be willing to aid him only because they'd want to make sure their betrotheds were kept safe since the ladies were determined to aid him, not so much because they wanted to right the wrong in his princedom.

"Where are we going?" Mirabella asked.

Argon rubbed his whiskery chin. "We will weigh anchor and meet with all the royals to determine the best course of action." He had to do that since they were willing to use their forces to help him and he knew they'd want to see their betrothed.

"Ah, good," Talamaya said, and Mexia agreed.

"Can you send word to Leogane that we are weighing anchor?" Argon asked Mexia.

"Aye." She hurried to the stern and once she was there, she waved her hands and cast a spell.

"What exactly are you doing?" Kersta said. "I've never seen you use this spell before."

"I think Derek is aiding me. The more I'm around him, the more I'm learning. I cast a spell to carry my voice to the person I wish to speak to and then his words are carried back to me."

"Oh, Leogane is weighing anchor too and joining you. He sounds eager to do so. Not to meet up with the other rulers, but to be with Mirabella." Kersta smiled at her as she joined them.

"Whoever would have thought I'd feel the same way about him," Mirabella said, leaning over the railing.

The other ships were sailing closer, and they had enough ships with just these to fight Zane, Argon thought.

It took a couple of hours before the other sailing ships were close enough to send transport boats with Lazarion and Derek to the Duchess, while Leogane visited with Mirabella.

Once the other men were on the Duchess, they all headed for Argon's captain's quarters. Argon hoped he could explain why he had taken the women hostage and that they would understand his need.

But instead of him, or King Lazarion speaking first when he outranked all of them, Kersta said, "I can read everyone's thoughts. Everyone has mixed feelings about this. But know this, we wanted to help Prince Argon in his quest to rescue his sister. It was the right thing to do. And helping him to take over his princedom is also meant to be."

"Aye," Talamaya agreed.

"I'm grateful to everyone who has come to my aid, the duke as well," Mirabella said. "And I understand you wish to help us deal with my murderous brother Zane as well."

Argon agreed and hoped they were understanding of the situation.

15

K ersta knew Argon was fraught with worry that the gathered royals would want to take him prisoner for what he had pulled with her and her companions. But she wanted them to know that at the end of this journey, the companions would return home and if her friends so wished it, they would wed their betrotheds. Of course, she should have made sure they agreed as well, but she said it just the same, wanting to help Argon and his sister out in the worst way. Though if Mirabella did marry Leogane, he would keep her safe from Zane, but Kersta knew they couldn't allow Zane to continue to rule.

"Princess Talamaya and Lady Mexia intend to marry their betrotheds at the end of this journey to free Prince Argon's people from Prince Zane's rule," Kersta said. "We cannot allow this prince who has murdered their father to get away with it. And if Argon hadn't escaped with his men on this ship, he would have been eliminated as well. But we have another issue also."

Lazarion had his arm wrapped around Talamaya's shoulder and he'd smiled down at her and kissed her upturned lips when he learned she was finally going to wed him and return to his kingdom. Likewise, if Derek had any notion of being angry over this whole fiasco, he had Mexia wrapped in his arms and looked well-pleased. The prophecy he had told them about would finally come true.

"What is this other thing?" Lazarion asked.

"Count Vladek. We're not sure who he is, or what he is. But he seems to be able to conjure up knights who, when we've killed them, turn to dust," Argon said. "He's tried to kill all of us countless times, hoping to grab my sister and take her back to Racine where he plans to marry her."

"Vladek of Racine, aye," Derek said. "He is a mage who uses black magic. He speaks with the dead and calls them into service when he needs to. He was a powerful third-year student at the mages' academy in Langston, but then he was expelled once he and two of his friends were found to be dabbling in the dark arts. Two of my friends and I found them raising the dead at a local cemetery. We had to report it. He was angry and sent the hoards after us. But we were even more powerful and sent the undead back to rest."

"A woman who worked for him said our mother was from there," Argon said and Kersta heard the worry in his words, that he was afraid she had also been a necromancer.

"Princess Xena? She had some innate magical ability, but not enough to make her a mage. She was all about good and light. She was a friend of my mother's, and my mother was glad she had married your father, but sorry to hear she had died shortly after Mirabella's birth. My mother lost touch with the family after that," Derek said.

Argon released a worried breath. Even Mirabella had been concerned about her mother's history. Kersta was glad it was all good.

"So can you help us fight both Count Vladek and Prince Zane?" Argon asked before Kersta could.

"Aye, I will. If we hadn't put down the hoards Vladek wielded against us, we would not be here sitting with you today. I would gladly put an end to the necromancer's evil ways." Derek glanced at Mirabella. "No way could we allow him to have you for a mate."

"I agree with that wholeheartedly," Mirabella said.

"Okay, about logistics?" Lazarion asked. "I have a hundred-and fifty-foot soldiers and knights on my ships."

"I'm carrying a hundred soldiers and three mages on mine," Derek said.

"I can call on more, but for now, I have thirty knights with me," Leogane said, sounding like his forces were puny in number compared to the other men's.

But Leogane hadn't known he was going to go to war, only that he was picking up a wife. And the element of surprise with so many gathered forces could work in their favor anyway.

"We will be a match for my brother's forces," Argon said. "But if we can reach Zane and his inner circle of friends without too much of a fight with Zane's forces, so much the better. Once I can eliminate the threat, hopefully the army and our naval forces will follow me."

"They will. Zane is a tyrant; you are not," Mirabella said.

"How will we manage to enter the seaport without Zane knowing we are there to oust him?" Leogane asked.

"He won't know that I would have the ability to rally troops on my behalf," Argon said. "I didn't know I would be able to either. We have many ships coming and going as they gather supplies and trade at the port. Your forces shouldn't be a concern as troop ships come though our seaports to gather supplies on long journeys and give the men a chance to stretch their legs."

"My mother will send men and ships if we need them," Talamaya said.

"She has already done so. Once I asked for word from you in Damar, she was just as concerned that you had not arrived on time. Naturally, we thought you had been caught up in the storm that we saw in the distance," Lazarion said.

That's when they saw Prince Grisom's ships—three more to add to their number.

"My twin brother is coming," Talamaya said, smiling.

Lazarion smiled. "See? We are all here for you."

"I propose that we take one each of our sailing ships near the harbor and send in the transport boats with whoever we need to make it look like we are there for shore leave and to buy supplies," Leogane said. "Naught more."

"And who will Argon travel with? The Duchess cannot be seen near the harbor," Lazarion said.

"Princess Mirabella should stay on the Duchess," Leogane said, "for her own safety."

"Argon will come with me," Derek said. He glanced at Mexia.

"I will as well."

"And me," Kersta said. "Unless you think the men on your ship cannot protect Mirabella." She remembered—belatedly—that she'd offered to protect her, but that was with the notion she would be traveling through the town.

"If Mirabella has no objection to this arrangement, she'll stay on the Duchess with my men and with Erlin," Argon said, glancing at Leogane to see if he was agreeable.

Leogane nodded.

"I have no objection. I'm not a fighter like the ladies, though I've been taught to defend myself. But if I went with all of you, I would put you in more danger should anyone recognize me. And, Argon, you need Kersta's help to protect you," Mirabella said.

Erlin said, "I will watch out for the princess."

"Where do ye intend to go?" Gallant asked Princess Talamaya.

"With her brother and me, our men, and you," King Lazarion said.

Gallant patted his war hammer. "Aye, that's what I was going to say, if she did not."

"What about the dragons," Mexia said. "They wanted to help."

"We'll call on them if we need their assistance," Argon said.

"I had an idea," Derek said. "Mexia and I and the other mages will cast an invisibility spell over us so we can find a way into the castle and hopefully reach your brother before any blood can be shed."

"I can use my invisibility cloak also," Kersta said. "I know it's unnecessary, but just in case."

"Sure. You're afraid our magic will fail, but it won't," Derek said. "But it doesn't hurt to feel safe. After we take care of your brother, we'll need to deal with Vladek. He won't want to let Mirabella go if he's decided she's going to be with him."

"I can't understand why he would want me," Mirabella said.

"You came of age and King Inari has offered an allegiance, lands, and gold for the one who marries you," Leogane said. "It was such a sudden thing that no one knew about it until the last minute."

"Because I wasn't Inari's to give until my brother murdered my father and Zane gave me to Inari to have me wed."

"Aye," Leogane said, taking her hand and squeezing it.

"Were you helping Mexia with her spells?" Kersta asked Derek.

"Aye. Or at least trying to aid her. I sensed she was in danger once I learned she wasn't in Damar. I saw the kishi in my mind's eye as if I were levitating them myself. I couldn't do the spell without her, but I was able to enhance hers so she could take them farther out to sea."

"Did you see what happened to them?" Mexia asked.

"Nay. No more than you could. When you let go of them, I didn't have any further control. Then when you were fighting the knights in black, I didn't know what to do. You were trying to attack them with your staff, but nothing was working. Unless you cast a spell, I couldn't aid you."

"What about when we were sleeping, and I protected my party with a protection spell?" Mexia asked.

"Aye. Though I have to admit my mage friends and I took turns keeping your barrier in place. We didn't want any of us to fall asleep and release our enhancement of the barrier should you have spent all your energy creating it in the first place."

"We all thank you for that," Talamaya said.

"Aye, ye did great," Gallant said.

"But again, I couldn't have created the spell to protect you in the first place. I could only help enhance it to take some of the burden off Mexia."

"And the swamp creatures?" Kersta asked. "You couldn't have helped Mexia levitate me all the way across the swamp when she and Argon had to fight the creatures?"

"Nay. Once Mexia couldn't concentrate on the spell, I couldn't cast it for you."

"Still, that's a remarkable feat none-the-less," Mexia said.

Everyone agreed.

They worked out more of the particulars and then finally they headed for Malaron and when they got to a safe distance from the harbor, the Duchess would be anchored and Kersta, Argon, and Mexia went to Derek's ship after everyone wished everyone well. Talamaya and Gallant were on Lazaron's ship, and he took the lead.

It was nightfall by the time they all reached the harbor and they weighed anchor. They were going to wait until morn to take the transport boats into shore, everyone preparing themselves mentally for a fight that night.

The male dragon fished for them again and brought fresh fish to each of the ships in addition to his own family.

Kersta was glad the dragon was aiding them in this way, since Argon didn't want him to help them in the fight, just yet. And hopefully they wouldn't need him. He had a family to take care of and resettle when the time and place was right.

She was glad they had so much help. She had thought they would try to slip in unnoticed, but with the mages' help, this would be so much better. Maybe they could take care of Zane and his cohorts and Argon would declare himself their ruler without any real fight. That's what she hoped for. They'd had to kill enough monsters. She sure didn't want to have to kill the men who could be loyal to Argon.

The ladies stayed in the captain's quarters that night and Mexia smiled at Kersta as they got ready to sleep. "You are marrying Argon, aren't you?"

"Aye. Whether he has a princedom or not. He can stay with me in the Kingdom of Damar if this doesn't work out for him there."

"You think he might not have his people's backs?"

"I don't know. If the people don't want to follow Argon, he can stay with me. Maybe we can even go adventuring." Kersta smiled, but she knew in her heart, Argon would feel bereft if he didn't free his people from Zane's rule and make him pay for murdering their father.

"Derek was amused you didn't trust in his spell to make you invisible." Mexia tucked her arms under her pillow.

"I guess you're right. I'm not used to being around him and his spells. You aid us all the time, Mexia. Without your abilities,

I'm not sure we would have made it through some of our quests."

"Nonsense. Each of you has been invaluable in solving these quests," Mexia said.

"But I want to have some control over my own destiny sometimes. So if I wear the cloak of invisibility, then I feel I will be taking care of myself while you and the other mages take care of anyone else who needs your assistance."

"We've been together for so many months, do you feel... adrift, so to speak, without Talamaya and Gallant here? In the beginning, I didn't think the disagreeable dwarf would last long with us, but you know through all of it, when others were deceptive, he's always been there for us," Mexia said.

"Aye, and I feel the same as you. I'm so used to Talamaya being with us and the three of us talking too long into the night, and Gallant covering his head with his backpack so he can muffle our voices even though we were speaking in hushed tones."

"I will miss that. He will stay with Talamaya in Malaron with King Lazarion, don't you agree?" Mexia asked.

"I would think so. Now that it looks as though I'm going to wed Argon, Gallant has no reason to entertain any notion I might be the one for him," Kersta said, laughing.

Mexia smiled. "He did have a crush on you. Does. I don't think he was too happy to learn you and Argon have hit it off so well. Mayhap someday, he will find just the right one for him. Someone who doesn't mind his trips to take on quests and earn some money."

"It would take someone special to put up with his gruff ways. Though I have to admit, he really grew on me."

"On all of us." Mexia closed her eyes and Kersta rolled over onto her back and closed hers.

"I do not look forward to tomorrow. I wish Talamaya was with us so we'd know what to expect if she has any visions."

"Aye, and then you could read her mind and tell me what she was seeing."

Then the women grew quiet and finally slept, only to be awakened at dawn.

"Time to eat, ladies," Derek said, as he and Argon walked into the captain's quarters. "'Tis time to get this journey under way.

16

Before they went to shore, Argon went with his sister to speak with Leogane, concerned about another issue. "What if Zane has had word that you have retrieved our sister from the Emerald Isle of Mists? He'll wonder why you are here and not taking her home to your own territory."

Leogane shook his head. "Nay. I've never met Zane and would use a different name while at the seaport, learning what I can, trading, and setting up for battle—just in case your plan to infiltrate the castle doesn't succeed."

Then that was at least settled.

Argon was torn between wanting to be with Kersta on the venture but wanting her to stay behind while they infiltrated the castle. She was not about to stay behind, however, and he understood her reasoning.

She had fought many a battle at her friends' sides and she wasn't about to sit this challenge out.

After they broke their fast with Derek and his mages, Mirabella hurried to give Kersta her short sword back. "I pray you won't have to use it." Then she gave her a hug.

Then Mirabella hugged Argon. "Do not get yourself killed over this. The princedom is not worth it."

But their brother had to pay for killing their father and for sending Mirabella to the Emerald Isle of Mists as a prisoner.

"I will do my best to right a wrong," Argon said, giving his sister a warm embrace and then he helped Kersta into the transport boat from Derek's ship. With sailors manning the oars, Derek and his mages and Kersta, Mexia, and Argon headed out, seeing King Lazarion, Princess Talamaya, and Gallant on another transport boat just docking now in the harbor.

Derek had turned Argon invisible for the trip and though Kersta wore the invisibility cloak and held Argon's hand, Mexia cast an invisibility spell on her as well, just in case. Though Argon was the only one at real risk should his people in the town or castle see him and recognize him.

Prince Grisom, Talamaya's brother, likewise, was in charge of his transport boat and he was behind Derek's.

Argon's hands were sweating and his heart pounding furiously. He knew no one could see him and he couldn't see Kersta, though he was glad she was holding his hand so he felt comforted to know she was sitting next to him. She leaned over and whispered to him, "If your people feel you are strong enough to overthrow your tyrant brother, they will support you."

"I pray that is so." He had too. He realized if he didn't win this battle, what could he even offer these different rulers in return for their help in the matter?

As if Derek could read minds, he said, "Do not worry about payment, Argon. 'Tis enough for me to be on this quest with Mexia."

They finally reached the dock and some of the soldiers left the boat first, then the mages left the boat, and finally, Argon climbed out and helped Kersta from the boat, though that was a feat in and of itself since he couldn't see her and no one else could either to aid him.

"Are we all accounted for?" Derek asked.

Argon slapped him on the back and Derek jumped a little, then smiled. "Show us the way then."

"To the right, down Water Street, turn right at Market Street and then up the hill to the castle. I'll lead you to a way to slip into the castle unseen beyond that." Argon took Kersta's hand. "I'll guide you with hushed words without spooking anyone who might hear me."

The castle and the seaport looked the same as always, Argon thought ruefully, as if nothing bad had gone on here recently. That no one cared that he and his sister or their father were gone.

The people were hardworking as usual, selling wares and doing chores like it was just any other day. He felt disappointed his father's death had no more impact on the people than that.

They began the trek toward the castle, Kersta still holding Argon's hand as they began the climb. The castle had been built on a granite hill overlooking the seaport town and to the west were forests they used to hunt in, to the east, grazing lands for cattle, sheep, and goats. Wild horses ran through the rolling grass hills farther way, and in the mountains, dragons lived in any number of caves. They didn't know how many made it their home, but they were content to live there in peace with the humans who had settled in the territory. They cared nothing about their politics, though Argon had considered going to stay in one of their caves had he not made it safely out of the town on the Duchess.

"Who tried to kill you?" Kersta whispered to him.

"Some of my brother's friends. I'm sure they were the ones who were on the hunt with him when he killed my father. There were three of them. A maid warned me they were coming for me. I grabbed a pack and my weapons. If I hadn't been armed, I would have been dead. I fought the three of them near the wharves when they caught up to me. But a runaway cart filled with produce raced down the cobblestone road headed straight for us as we crossed swords. If it hadn't been for that, I wouldn't have made it."

"A runaway cart? Accidental? Or on purpose?"

"On purpose, I like to believe. In any event, my brother's assassins jumped out of the path of the cart, and I managed to slip away down another street. Then I finally made my way to the dock and a waiting transport boat and was rowed out to the Duchess. They had just loaded provisions and told me they were waiting for me."

"How did they know you needed to sail somewhere?"

"They'd learned my sister was taken hostage in the night and they knew I would be searching for her as soon as I returned from my peacekeeping mission."

"Then someone was looking out for you." Kersta squeezed his hand.

"Aye. My bos'n mate had taken charge, made sure the ship was ready to sail, and intended to come for me to ensure I made it to the ship all right. He was on the Duchess when he saw my brother's friends fighting me."

"And no one helped?" Kersta sounded angry.

"Except for the runaway cart. No one in town could fight three armed knights. They're just merchants and such. No one armed or trained for combat. Not to mention the men were friends of my brother's, and lords."

"Aye, I see."

Then they continued on in silence, but before they reached the gates, Argon seized Derek's shoulder. "We go right here. There's no trail at all, but it leads to the escape tunnels into the castle. That's how I left when I learned my brother planned to have me killed."

They paused and glanced around. The men on the high castle wall walk couldn't see them for the trees here, but as soon as they went the way Argon told them too, they would be visible.

"Cast the spell of invisibility," Derek whispered, and then all of them vanished.

They all held hands to make their way in the same direction as Argon was traveling. Argon was used to good old-fashioned fighting, so subterfuge wasn't really his way. But if it meant he'd keep the rest of his people safe, he would do anything.

As soon as they reached a cave far from the castle walls, he came to a locked metal door and unlocked it, then they all went inside, and he locked the door again. The problem was they needed light.

"I'll cast a fairy light," Mexia said. "We can extinguish it if we hear anyone coming."

They had to use the light, though if anyone came upon them, all they'd see was the light and nobody holding it.

"No one comes down here. No one but the royal family knew of its existence," Argon said. "Our father showed us the way years ago when we were young."

They continued on their way, each holding hands through the maze of tunnels. It would be easy to lose one's way in here and he wanted to make sure that everyone stayed together. He wished they could see each other. It was just eerie to hear light footsteps every once in a while, a kicked stone clunking against the rock wall, a splash of water when someone stepped into a pothole filled with water. Water dripped incessantly down the cave walls, and everything glistened in the soft glow of Mexia's light.

Bats twittered nervously way above them.

"You know the way, aye?" Derek asked, sounding worried they were lost since they had traveled so far.

Argon wondered if Derek didn't like enclosed spaces. "Aye. It would not make for a good escape tunnel if it was too easy for an enemy to find the entrance and make their way inside to the castle."

Then they finally saw a faint light around a square object.

"Each of the royal bedchambers had a secret passage into the maze of tunnels. This one leads to my father's chamber."

"What if your brother is staying there now?" Kersta asked.

"That's what I was thinking." Then Argon opened the square metal door and pushed a chest aside to enter the room. He had thought of going to his own room, or his brother's, but his brother might have given their rooms to a couple of his loyal friends, and he didn't want to start a fight with them and alert Zane and his loyal guards prematurely.

As soon as they entered the bedchamber, the mages all looked at each other in shock. So did Argon. Only Kersta, wearing her invisibility cloak, was invisible.

"Your spells wore off?" Argon asked, his words hushed. This was a disaster. Instead of having armed knights with him, he was with a bunch of lightly armed mages whose real power came from magic, not weapons!

Mexia looked panicked and tried to move a candle sitting on top of a chest with her levitation spell, but nothing happened.

"I didn't think you and your family had any mages working for you," Derek said. "Was I mistaken?"

"Nay. We have never hired mages here." Argon wondered if his brother had learned he had kidnapped Mexia and thought he might bring her back here to fight his battles and so had hired a mage to work for him.

"'Tis magic, all right," Derek said. "A mage has removed any mage's ability to cast magic in this room. Mayhap even in the entire castle."

"Like you had done at your castle in Albion to prevent me from casting my magic," Mexia said to Derek. "Is there no way to counteract it?"

"Only by killing the mage who constructed the spell," Derek said.

They heard footfalls headed in their direction, though whoever it was could be on an errand that would take them past the chamber. All the mages and Argon scurried back into the secret tunnel to hide, and he assumed Kersta had come with them. But when he shut the door and they heard the door open to the chamber, he whispered to Kersta, and she was not among them.

He was ready to leave the safety of the tunnel and kill whoever it was, even though Kersta was still invisible due to her cloak and was safe enough, he thought.

"Hurry. Change the sheets. King Lazarion and his queen will be staying here. And we must change the linens in Princess Mirabella's chamber so that Prince Zane can move there until his honored guests leave. King Lazarion was very gracious and didn't want to trouble anyone, which is unusual to say the least. But Prince Zane insisted. I suspect he is hoping to make a good impression on the king from the continent of Inherian and maybe gain an alliance. We must change the linens in Prince Argon's chamber as well since Count Vladek will be staying there the night. Or several. Who knows?"

Argon barely breathed at hearing the woman's words.

Derek whispered to him, "If Count Vladek is here already, he very well could have cast spells to protect the castle from any other magic user in the vicinity from being able to cast one."

Then Argon had even more of a reason to kill the count. What if he raised the dead from their cemeteries, or if Argon's new allies fought and any of the people died, they were used as part of Vladek's new forces?

Mexia had a belt that could reflect the spell cast by another at her, which could be used as a last resort. Gallant wore a helm that protected him from a spell caster's ability to force him to do his bidding. And for now, though Argon was really sweating this out, Kersta was hidden by her invisibility cloak.

"I worry about Princess Mirabella," one of the maids said.

"Aye, do not speak of it," the other said.

"I pray she is all right."

"What did I say?"

"I...I wanted to tell Prince Argon she had been stolen away—"

"Listra, hush. You will be the death of us."

"I didn't have time." Listra took a deep breath. "But I did warn the prince to leave."

They were changing the linens and then the other woman said, "I know. I know. But dinna let anyone else learn of it. Some will do anything to stay on Prince Zane's good side for power and glory, ye know. Ye best let it go, because if Prince Zane hears of it, ye will be dead for sure. And for all we know, Prince Argon is gone forever, never to return. So it does us no good to think upon it."

KERSTA WANTED in the worst way to tell these women that Prince Argon intended to free their people from Prince Zane's rule, assuming they were on Argon's side. But what could the women do about anything?

Though men oft believed that women who served in subservient roles weren't as much of a threat, when they truly could be, working behind the scenes to rally the people in

Argon's favor. But it could all backfire too, if they told the wrong person who was loyal to Zane and would hurry to tell him about any such plot for a reward. There were always those who would stab their own brother in the back if it meant they would gain something for it.

"Come on, hurry and help me finish his lordship's bed," the older of the two women said.

Then the older woman left the room and the other—the one who had warned Argon to leave before Zane's men killed him— was gathering up the rest of the dirty linens when Kersta left the chamber, saw the hall was clear, removed her cloak, and walked back into the chamber as if she was just part of the staff there. Though she was armed with a staff and her sword—glad Mirabella had returned it to her in case she needed it.

Listra gasped.

"I'm here to tell you that Prince Argon and his sister are alive and well. In two weeks' time, they will be here to free the castle of Zane's tyranny. Tell all who are loyal to Argon that this will come to pass."

"Who, what..."

"I must leave. Where is Vladek staying?"

"In Prince Argon's chamber."

"Thanks be to thee. Just do not tell the wrong person this news." Even though Kersta had stated it would be much later than the intended battle, telling the wrong person could cause more problems for them. She worried Argon would be upset with her for speaking to the woman, but once the mages' magic wouldn't work, they had to come up with another plan. And she and her companions had been doing that for months.

"You have a staff and short sword very similar to Queen Tala-maya's," the woman observed.

Kersta couldn't believe Talamaya was claiming to be the king's wife, but to stay safe and remain together, she could understand that. "These are dangerous times. Many women who are traveling are so armed. Do you know if Vladek has anything with him he uses to focus his magic with?" Kersta knew some mages used a focusing stone if they were to cast lots of magic spells at the same time. Maybe, if he didn't carry it with him, they could destroy it and the mages could regain their use of magic.

"Mayhap. There's a glowing, round, amethyst orb that sits in Prince Argon's chamber. It might have a protection spell on it so no one attempts to steal it. Though everyone's afraid to go near it."

"Thank you."

The woman quickly curtseyed and then grabbed up the dirty linens and hurried out of the chamber.

Kersta turned invisible and headed for the secret door. She'd been torn between following the maid out of the room and trying to learn who all was loyal to Argon or hiding with him in the secret tunnels. But they couldn't hide there forever. They needed to destroy Zane, his inner circle of friends, and Count Vladek and his friends as soon as they could.

17

"Did you hear what was said?" Kersta asked as she crept through the tunnel maze to Argon's old chamber, hoping Argon and the others weren't angry with her for taking her own initiative to forge a plan without their consent.

"Aye. Vladek has a focusing stone. I cannot believe he is here, in league with my brother. We must destroy the stone," Argon said.

"We cannot destroy it, but we can send it to a watery grave," Derek said.

"Like we did with Grimoria," Mexia added.

"Oh, aye, we can take it far out to sea, but will it sink?" Kersta asked.

"It might float," Derek said. "And it would take too long to sail away with it to dump it safely far enough from Vladek's grasp."

"The dragon. He could fly it far out to sea, and it wouldn't take him as long as a ship would, sailing in the rough waters," Kersta said. "But if it floats—"

"What if I turned it to stone?" Mexia asked. "A heavy enough rock would make it sink."

"Let's try it. The problem would be if Vladek has a protection spell on it, and also a beacon that would tell him where it is," Derek said. "Though if it were deep enough in the sea, the necromancer would never be able to retrieve it. No one would."

"If we can get rid of it, and you can get the use of your magic back, it will be worth trying," Argon said.

"We might not get the use of our magic back, but it could limit his use of spells," Derek said.

"Okay, I had another idea. I can make the region go back to an earlier time. What if we are here before Vladek arrives? Then we can take him down as soon as he turns up. But in the meantime, Prince Zane wouldn't have the use of Vladek's magic," Mexia said. "It won't affect us, only those in the castle. As long as your brother and his friends and Vladek are in the castle at the time, it would work."

"But you can't cast any spell unless we get rid of his focusing stone, first," Derek said. "If it's in his chamber, I'll grab it. I don't want anyone else hurt if it is protected by a spell that will injure or kill."

"What if you hit it with your staff, knock it into the tunnels, and Mexia can turn it to stone?" Kersta asked.

"It's worth a try," Mexia said.

When they reached Prince Argon's secret chamber door, they listened to any sound coming from there and heard a man talking to another in there.

"I don't understand why King Inari gave Duke Leogane the opportunity to take Princess Mirabella for his wife. The deal you made with Prince Zane was that King Inari would offer her to you and only you, Count Vladek."

"I will deal with the king later. What I don't like is for some king from another continent gaining all Zane's favor while I'm here, as if I no longer matter in the scheme of things. He had better watch who he allies with. No one wants to get on my bad side. Being emperor over all the regions won't happen soon enough for me," Count Vladek said.

A knock sounded on the bed chamber door and then the door opened.

"Beg your pardon, Count Vladek, but we're here to change your bed linens," the older woman said. "We didn't have time before you arrived. If you want us to return until later, we can."

"Nay. Do it now. Come on, Greaves."

"That's one of the mages Vladek was working with as a necromancer in the cemetery in Langdon," Derek whispered. "Salton, is the other."

"This presents a problem. We didn't realize Vladek was doing business with my brother. If it's true Vladek and some of his men were with Leogane on his journey to pick up Mirabella, then Vladek does know who Leogane is," Argon said.

"Oh, also all of us. Mexia, Gallant, Talamaya even. Unless he left before we arrived at the camp," Kersta said.

"What about him sending his dark knights after us?" Mexia asked. "Wouldn't he know we were working with Argon to free his sister?"

"Mayhap he hasn't seen Talamaya and Gallant there just yet. Though I wonder, did he know that's who she was and that's why they were invited to the castle? Keep your friends close and your enemy closer comes to mind," Kersta said.

"Then we have to get in there and protect them," Argon said.

Kersta wished they could have just eliminated the two mages right then and there, but without being able to cast magic spells, that would have been a disaster for her and her friends.

As soon as the maids finished changing the linens in Prince Argon's room, the door closed with a clunk and Argon opened the secret door into his former chamber.

Kersta had been afraid the mage would have taken the focusing crystal with him, but it was sitting on a table next to the canopied bed. She handed her cloak to Derek so he could wear it and if the count could "see" someone approach the crystal, he wouldn't be able to observe Derek.

Once she gave up her cloak to him though, Kersta felt vulnerable, and she realized how much she depended on having it with her.

Mexia handed her specially enhanced staff to Derek also, just in case his own staff couldn't protect him.

Then under the invisibility cloak, Derek moved into the room, taking much longer than Kersta thought wise. But maybe he was trying to identify any magic traps the count might have set up.

Then with a whack! He struck the crystal orb and sent it flying through the air and into the tunnels where Argon caught it and set it on the cave floor. The mages surrounded it in a hiding spell, in case Vladek could sense it with his magic.

"No protection spell on the gem. I forgot how truly arrogant he is." Derek shut the secret door to the chamber and handed the cloak to Kersta. "Which is to our advantage."

Mexia quickly cast a spell, turning the beautiful purple gem into a solid stone of periodotite—a dark-colored, olive green, igneous rock. "It's one of the heaviest rocks there are," she said.

"One of us needs to get this to the dragon," Derek said.

"I'll go," Mexia said. "I can use my magic here in the tunnels and outside the cave."

Derek looked reluctant to let her go in the event she ran into any trouble, but Kersta suspected he wanted to stay here to deal with Vladek.

"I'll go," Dragonmage said. He grabbed the stone ball and transported outside the tunnels without hesitation and could do so now that they'd been through the maze.

"Now what do we do?" Kersta asked.

"Let us return to my father's chamber and once inside, see if you can cast spells now inside the castle," Argon said.

It certainly was worth a try, though Kersta was afraid Vladek could still conjure up his own spells even without his powerful focusing stone.

Once they reached the door to Argon's father's chamber, they heard conversation in there. What now? But then Kersta realized the people speaking were Lazarion and Talamaya.

"Remember, since we are not married—yet—we do not sleep together," Talamaya said.

"You are not sleeping alone," Lazarion said.

"Gallant will be right outside the door."

"Aye, and I will be right next to you."

Then they stopped talking and Kersta opened the door and saw the two kissing. Lazarion swung around, pulling his sword. Talamaya had readied her staff, then both smiled with relief to see them all there—Argon, Kersta, Mexia, and the mages, all but one.

"You're staying the night?" Kersta asked, still surprised at the change in events.

"Aye, down at the docks the word spread we were royalty, and they sent a greeting party to bring us to the castle. We're going down to a royal feast in celebration. But we have to warn you, Count Vladek is also here," Talamaya said.

"Aye, we are in the process of eliminating his focusing stone," Derek said, casting a spell and making the bed levitate. "Good. Vladek had cast a spell that had prevented our using magic. We had to get rid of the focusing crystal."

"Vladek could very well know you, that you fought his knights when we were on the Emerald Isle of Mists," Argon said to Talamaya.

"We were worried about that. But because I'm with Lazarion,

I don't believe Vladek realizes I am one and the same as the woman who was fighting dark knights on the Emerald Isle of Mists. Most unusual to be a queen and doing so, wouldn't you say?"

"Aye," Mexia and Kersta agreed.

A knock sounded on the door and Derek and Mexia waved their hands and all their party vanished.

"Aye, come," Lazarion said.

The door opened and a man inclined his head. "I'm to escort you to the meal."

"Tala," Lazarion said, offering his arm to her, and then she settled her arm on his, smiled at him, and the two left the chamber, the lord escorting them, shutting the door behind him.

Then each of the mages tried to use their magic—one of them made the wardrobe chest disappear, then brought it back. Another created a griffin in the chamber, and everyone was prepared to fight it, but then the mage snapped his fingers and the griffin disappeared.

"An illusion," Mer said. "I'm a master of illusions."

"You should have told us before you nearly gave everyone a heart attack," Kersta said. "Now what do we do?"

"I want to hear what is being said at the meal, to see if we can set up an ambush for my brother and his men," Argon said.

"And Vladek and his men. The inner circle of necromancers and dark royals who have killed or attempted to kill those in power," Derek said.

"But we must be silent, no speaking at all. I can read minds and when we're done in the great hall, we can return to King Lazarion and Talamaya's chamber," Kersta said.

"If anyone encounters any trouble at all, retreat to the tunnel," Argon said. "My brother would not tell Vladek or his mages, or his own friends either about the tunnels. We should be safe there."

Then they all agreed and headed for the great hall, all invisible, careful to avoid running into anyone. They could not be seen, but if anyone were to touch them in the same space, they could feel something solid and cry out in fright, alerting the guards and the mages, who might suspect something was wrong.

It was nerve-wracking going down to the great hall like this, not being able to see anyone else in their group, knowing only that Argon was in the lead, his hand on Kersta's as they headed down the stairs, then suddenly had to flatten themselves against a wall as a servant ran up the stairs.

They continued to descend to the bottom of the steps until they reached a grand entryway and Argon led them into the great hall.

Kersta felt Mexia bump into her and Kersta smiled. Then Argon pulled Kersta away with him toward the head table. She had no idea where anyone else would be, but she stayed with Argon until they were standing behind his brother, and she imagined he wished he could end his life right then and there.

Vladek was sitting to the right of Zane. Lazarion was seated on Zane's left, and Talamaya next to the king on his left.

Kersta quieted her mind and began to listen to the words in people's thoughts.

Suddenly, a dozen men came into the great hall, and they were dark knights! This was so not good. They were the undead, right? Then they couldn't eat. What purpose had they in coming to the meal?

Argon touched her arm and ran his hand down to hers and took hold and squeezed.

That's when she heard Vladek's thoughts. *"Good. You are here. How many of our men are here?"*

He wasn't just thinking the thoughts. He was communicating

with his knights telepathically, and she realized she could read them also.

"A hundred knights are now taking quarter at various houses in the village as you have commanded."

Kersta was dying to warn Argon and the others what was going on.

Then Zane leaned over to speak to Lazarion. "What brought you to our seaport?"

Kersta stiffened, afraid of what the king might say.

"My wife was visiting with friends and I'm returning her to her family, then we're going back home."

"Where is her family?"

"The kingdom of Damar."

Zane rubbed his whiskered chin. "If you ever have need of an alliance, I would be willing to draw up a treaty with you."

King Lazarion cast him a small smile. "Are you allied with King Inari?"

Zane leaned back in his chair and frowned. "Aye. He is my uncle. Why?"

"I had intended to speak to him about an alliance. I suppose if I ally with him, I will be allied with you, since he is your uncle. Who is Count Vladek to you?"

"Uh, an ally."

Kersta heard Talamaya whisper to Lazarion, "Tell him the knights shouldn't be at the meal if they're not eating. They're the dark knights we encountered on the Emerald Isle of Mists. They're the undead."

Lazarion's eyes darkened and he inclined his head to Talamaya, then turned to speak to Zane again. "Count Vladek's men seem...rather unusual. They sit at the meal, yet do not partake of it. They haven't even removed their helms or weapons. Forgive me for saying so, but it makes me feel as though your castle is under siege."

Zane glanced at the dark knights. "I...agree."

Why hadn't he noticed this before? Or realized how hostile the knights seemed to be?

Zane turned to speak with Vladek and that worried Kersta. What if Vladek decided to order his knights to kill everyone they could in the great hall right now?

"Can you tell your knights to leave? If they are not eating, they're making my guests uncomfortable with their presence," Zane said to Vladek.

Did the prince not know Vladek was a necromancer, and his knights were undead? He was a fool.

"Who wishes it?" Vladek asked, glancing around Zane to glower at Lazarion.

"The king is right in saying your knights are not eating the meal prepared for us. They look like they're ready to fight instead." Zane stiffened his back, sounding annoyed that this was *his* princedom and Vladek didn't just do what he requested. "Aren't you supposed to be finding my sister and taking her to your home in Racine?"

Vladek gave him an evil smile. "I will do just that, when the time is right."

Kersta wanted to do something in the worst way, kill these men at once, but not with all the undead knights here who could hurt the unarmed civilians seated at the tables throughout the great hall.

It would be better—as much as it didn't seem very civil—to kill these men in their beds as they slept, then no harm would come to the innocents. Though she suspected they didn't sleep.

"Very well," Vladek said, but he didn't sound happy about it. *"Take the men and find quarters in the village for the rest of them. We will gather tonight at the castle once the prince and his guests have retired for the night,"* he told his men, speaking telepathically again.

Kersta sure wished she could speak with her friends in such a manner.

But she realized that was when Vladek planned to take over the princedom. He would kill King Lazarion and Princess Talamaya in their beds tonight, if he could. He would eliminate Prince Zane and his cohorts too. Well, he was free to do that, but the problem with that was that Vladek had so many knights that they could kill whoever he wanted them to. She could read his mind, to her surprise, but he didn't seem to know Talamaya had been on the journey to free Mirabella. Talamaya was most likely correct. Vladek probably wouldn't have thought she was one of the women working for Argon, not when she was married to a king and was with the king there now.

When Vladek retired to his chamber, he would learn someone had taken his focusing crystal and she was afraid what would happen then. She could imagine him killing any number of servants, thinking one of them had stolen it.

The dark knights left the great hall then and Kersta breathed a sigh of relief.

Talamaya did too. Kersta wondered if she'd had any visions at all about what was going to take place.

Then Talamaya was thinking that they needed to warn their men in town about the dark knights. They needed to destroy the dark knights while they were at the houses. They needed to get word to Leogane, if he hadn't seen the dark knights, that Vladek and his men were there.

Kersta pulled at Argon's hand, telling him wordlessly they needed to leave at once. She took him back to his father's chamber and they entered it, then slipped into the safety of the tunnels.

"What's wrong?" Argon asked.

She told him what Talamaya had been thinking. "I believe she figured I might be nearby her and listening to everyone's thoughts, including hers. I have to warn Talamaya's brother, Lazarion's men, and Leogane about the dark knights. I have to warn Derek's knights. Our allies all know me, but your people do not. Except for the sailors on the ship. So I can slip away and find the men and tell them what must be done. You have to stay here and fight Vladek and your brother and their cohorts. You have to let the others know what I'm doing. We have to eliminate the dark knights before Vladek can use them to take over your castle."

Argon pulled Kersta into a heartfelt hug. "If I could send anyone else, or go myself, I would do it. But you are right. We have to warn the others right away and I must stay here and tell the mages and Talamaya and Lazarion what is happening. Go. Be careful. Trust no one but our own people."

"I have my cloak. If I get myself into trouble, I'll disappear."

He kissed her mouth. "I love you. Stay safe."

"I love you too. Don't you dare get yourself killed either." Then she kissed him back and she sighed. "I can't transport out of here like the mages can. And I will lose my way if I try to leave on my own."

"I will take you to the exit." He hurried her all the way through the maze and when they reached the locked door, she realized he would have had to come with her anyway because she didn't have the key. He unlocked it for her, and she hugged him again and then left. She wore the cloak all along the path until she was in the woods, then turned it so she was no longer invisible. She ran into the mage returning from his errand with the dragon and he was surprised to see her.

She quickly explained the trouble and what they needed to do. "Did you get the stone to the dragon?"

"Aye. He was eager to help and flew with it out to sea. I'm going with you to help spread the word."

"All right. We can go our separate ways and find whoever we

can, to tell them what needs to be done." She prayed that when they went to the houses, the dark knights would not kill the families living in them. "We must eliminate the dark knights before nightfall, or whenever Vladek intends to have them enter the castle."

18

Kersta and Dragonmage hurried through the woods until they came to a street and headed down to the wharves. Dragonmage soon saw some of Derek's men and they looked surprised to see him returning so soon.

"You speak with them. I see Talamaya's brother going into that weapon's shop. I'll tell him what's going on." Kersta hurried off to meet up with Grisom. When she reached the shop, she went inside to see the prince looking at swords.

She joined him and whispered, "I need to speak with you at once."

The prince knew she was worried and took her arm and led her back outside. "What's wrong?"

She quietly said, "Vladek is here with his dark knights allied with Zane—for the moment. But he intends to kill Zane and your sister and Lazarion also tonight while they're sleeping."

Grisom started to move in the direction of the castle, and she quickly grabbed his arm and stopped him. "Wait. The mages and Argon will protect them. Not that your sister doesn't do a great job of taking care of herself, but the dark knights are quartered in homes all over the city. We need to find the dark knights and destroy them before the count can call on them to do his bidding. We must warn the others with us and do this now."

"All right."

Then she and Grisom took off in different directions, Grisom to tell some of his men, all of whom she knew from Damar, even her three suitors who smiled and waved at her. They must not have gotten word she already had thrown them over for a prince. She saw Leogane at the fish market and hurried off to warn him of the news.

Once she told him what was going on, she said, "Now that you know Vladek is here, do you think you should return to your ship?"

"Nay. My men and I will help to kill the knights before they can do anyone any harm. Mirabella will never be safe until we eliminate the necromancers and their forces."

"I agree." Then she saw the men all gathering together and heading down the streets, but they disappeared into the family gardens or back alleys. She suspected they were going to enter through a back door or window so they wouldn't cause speculation if so many men were seen suddenly knocking on front doors. Even so, as they slipped through garden gates, they appeared to be talking and laughing with their friends as if they were expected and they weren't ready to kill some undead knights.

Then Leogane was at Kersta's side, and Dragonmage joined them too. "We know you're not going to stay out of this, so we'll go together," Leogane said.

She smiled at him.

The duke shrugged. "I'm marrying your soon to be sister-in-law. We'll be family. I'm not letting you do this on your own."

"Derek is my best friend. He's marrying one of your best friends, Mexia. Neither would forgive me if I wasn't there to ensure you made it through this all right either," Dragonmage said.

"Okay, first house on the left then. Front door or—" she asked.

"Front door," Leogane said.

She wasn't surprised the duke would want to make more of a grand entrance. The mage agreed and vanished. She took Leogane's hand and he looked down at her. "We're pretending to be a couple so it doesn't look like we're on a warrior's mission, despite how armed we both are."

"Right." Leogane knocked on the door.

She wondered if Dragonmage was still with them, or if he was slipping in a back way to aid them before the fight.

A small, black-haired girl wearing pigtails answered the door, her big, brown eyes round as she stared up at them.

Kersta wasn't thinking that a young girl would answer the door. "Where is your mother?"

"She is the tailor and she's working on the mending."

"Do you have brothers and sisters?" Kersta asked, needing the kids and mother out of the house now.

"A sister."

"Go get your sister and come out here. I have a game to show you," Kersta said.

The girl looked wary.

"Hurry. And then my husband wishes to speak to your mother about some mending we need done."

"Aye." The girl dashed off, leaving the door wide open and Kersta and Leogane walked into the house.

The girl quickly told her mother that the visitors needed some mending done. And then she grabbed her little sister's hand and headed for the door.

"Aye?" the woman said, looking over Leogane and Kersta.

Kersta figured she was calculating how much to charge him because he was dressed so well.

"I've just come from my ship"—Leogane motioned to the door—"and we have a couple of pounds worth of clothing that need repair. Would you come outside and take a look at them and give me a price?"

"Aye, I will." The woman and her two daughters went outside, but she looked confused when she saw no pile of clothes that needed mending.

Leogane quickly asked, "How many knights are quartering in your house?"

"Three." Here dark eyes growing huge, the woman looked alarmed.

Leogane inclined his head. "Stay here with the children. Unless there is someplace else you can go for safety. Someplace these knights are not quartering."

"Everyone has been forced to take them in," the woman said.

"Stay here," Leogane said again, then stalked off for the door.

"I will show you girls a game when I return. I must help him." Then Kersta rushed after Leogane, needing to fight the knights too. As soon as she entered the house, they saw the three knights in a separate room.

They rose to their feet and Leogane immediately cut off one of the dark knight's heads, Kersta rammed her staff into the chest of another and he disintegrated into ash, only his armor—with a hole in the chest—left behind.

The other dark knight crumpled onto the floor. Dragonmage made himself visible and said, "You didn't tell us they needed to be stabbed in the heart or beheaded."

"Oh, no, I didn't." Kersta headed out of the house. Then she saw the little girls waiting for her to show them a game and she recalled the dead knights were in their house. Too many things on her mind. Mainly—to get rid of the knights before they could warn Vladek and before they could hurt anyone.

"She will come back later to play a game with you," the woman said, acknowledging Kersta with an incline of her head.

"The knights are...uhm, ashes, but their armor is still there. You can salvage what you can and sell it. We must help others to help rid the town of these dark knights," Kersta said.

"Ashes?" The woman looked a little gray herself.

"Aye." Kersta leaned over and whispered to the women, not wanting the young girls to hear her. "The undead. Count Vladek is a necromancer. He is evil to the core."

"Thanks be to thee for helping us," the woman said.

"Aye, we were glad to."

"My brother lives on Wayfarer Street with his wife and four young children. Can you see to them too?"

"Aye. To everyone."

"It's the home with the blue door. He's a fisherman. He would never be able to fight these knights."

"We will see to it." Then Kersta and the mage and Leogane hurried off to the next house, but three of Derek's knights were coming out of that one.

"You could have told us they had to be struck in the heart," one of the men said to Kersta and Leogane.

"Or beheaded," Leogane said. "We need to spread the word."

"What did you do to the knight?" Kersta asked the Dragonmage.

"I used my power to squeeze his heart until it burst. You would not think the undead would have a heart."

"Aye. I agree." She and Leogane and the mage hurried off to Wayfarer Street and finally found the house with the blue door. "Should we attempt entry the same way as before?"

"Aye, it worked well for us." Leogane knocked on the door.

The mage vanished.

Kersta took Leogane's hand as a man called out, "We are busy eating. Come back later."

"Your sister and her two little girls have had a fire in the house. They need your help. We put out the fire, but they need to move in with—" Kersta quit speaking when a man yanked open the door.

"Are they all right?" the young bearded man asked.

"Aye. They could use your help and the kids', and your wife needs to come too. The girls are scared and won't leave the house, though it is no longer safe there," Kersta said.

"What is this all about?" a woman asked, a toddler on her hip, three little boys clinging to her skirts.

"His sister"—whom Kersta didn't know the name of!—"has had a fire. She and the children need your help."

The woman narrowed her eyes at Kersta. "Why would she be needing me to bring my little ones to her house?"

"She wants you to live," Kersta said, her voice lowered, angry. "Go, now, while we kill the dark knights in your home."

The woman's eyes grew huge. Her husband didn't have to be told twice and grabbed up the two youngest ones clinging to his wife's skirts and headed for his sister's house. The wife grabbed the last son's hand and hurried off after her husband.

"What if they just want to steal from us once we left?" the woman complained to her husband.

"Ye saw how they are dressed. They are people of some means and they're armed. If they rid us of those knights, so much the better," the husband said. "And ye think they are going to steal from us with those knights in the house anyway?" He cast an annoyed glance at her.

Leogane and Kersta entered the house and saw three knights seated at the table, or their armor was, cards on the table, some scattered to the wooden floor, heads, or ash-filled helms, resting on the table.

The mage appeared, dusting off his hands as if he'd gotten them dirty. "That was easy, once I knew how to eliminate them."

"Good." But then they saw five dark knights riding toward the castle and that was not good. "What if they have had word about us killing the other dark knights and they're heading to the castle to warn Vladek?" Kersta said.

"Or he's already told them to join him at the castle. The sun is beginning to set," Leogane warned.

They chased after the knights, but they'd never be able to catch up to them on foot. "Can't you do something?" Kersta asked Dragonmage. They needed to stop them now!

"I can't—wait..." Then Dragonmage smiled and cast a spell. A rock wall suddenly appeared in front of the knights. The three knights in the lead veered off to the left. The ones behind them had enough time to rein in their horses and stop.

A cart full of fruits and vegetables hurtled toward all of them and the horses reared up, the three knights tumbling from their horses. If only Kersta and the others could reach them before they recovered their horses.

The last two knights whipped around to fight Leogane and Kersta. Dragonmage had vanished.

Kersta didn't have time to use her cloak to make herself invisible. She dodged out of the charging knight's path. She'd meant to fight one on foot, not one still seated on his horse.

He swung low with his sword to hit her. She parried, hit his broadsword hard with her staff, knocking it out of his hand. She figured he hadn't expected that.

He leapt down from his horse. Good. Now she was at more of an advantage. Though he wouldn't think so. He came at her, a short sword in hand and she used her staff in defense, blocking his every thrust, his every slash while she heard others fighting the dark knights. This was not good. Word would reach the other knights, she feared, and they'd be in for a big fight.

Which was just what happened. Fighting was going on in every street, but what shocked her most was the villagers were fighting the dark knights with pitchforks, forcing them off their horses. Once the dark knights were unseated from their mounts, Derek's, Leogane's, Grisom's, and Lazarion's men were going in for the kill.

But then a group of knights rode down from the castle, wearing the tunic that Argon wore. "Oh, no, oh, no, Zane's men are reinforcing the knights!" she shouted, needing desperately to drink Modi's tea for strength, or to just end this fight with the dark knight, but neither she nor the dark knight seemed to be making any progress and she was wearing down.

Then out of the corner of her eye, she saw the little girl who had answered the door to Kersta, and she was running toward her. "Stay back!" Kersta shouted to her.

That was just the distraction the dark knight needed to get the advantage in this fight with Kersta.

Right after the meal at the castle, Argon and the others gathered with Lazarion and Talamaya in their chamber. Argon explained what Kersta had gone to do and that if they were successful, the party here would only have to eliminate Vladek and his necromancer friends and Zane and his friends.

But Argon kept worrying about Kersta.

"She has never failed us once," Gallant said, as if he knew just how Argon was feeling.

The mage Fessenwig made the bureau disappear again. "Just making sure the focusing stone isn't here again."

"They are in a great battle," Talamaya said. "It's spilled out into the streets everywhere."

"Then we have to do what we've come to do. No more waiting," Argon said, but he paused for consensus to ensure everyone was doing this too.

"Your brother has sent forces to quell the uprising," Talamaya warned. "I saw it in a vision." She readied her scepter. "Guards are on their way to arrest King Lazarion and me now."

"Let them come," Argon said.

And then Derek and the other mages turned everyone except for the king and Talamaya invisible.

A pounding on the door shook it hard—not a maid's light touch, but a guard's that said he was ready to enforce his lord's orders.

The door opened and two men stood there—guards who Argon knew.

"You must come with us," the one guard said.

"No," Argon said, forgetting he was invisible.

The guards had started to step into the chamber, but both swung around to see where the voice was coming from. "Prince Argon?" the one guard said.

The other looked white as a ghost.

"Zane killed our father and kidnapped our sister and imprisoned her on the Emerald Isle of Mists." Argon was hoping one of the mages with him would turn him visible again, but nobody did. Maybe the mages thought he had more impact on the guards as a spirit. "And he tried to have me murdered."

"Tried," the one guard said, exchanging glances with the other, most likely figuring Zane had succeeded.

"He speaks the truth," Talamaya said. "We helped rescue Princess Mirabella and freed her from the tower at the castle on the Emerald Isle of Mists."

The guards' jaws dropped. "You're here to do what?" the one asked.

"What do you think? Zane has offered to give Mirabella to a necromancer. A mage who raises the dead. Vladek. Count

Vladek. The man who has dead dark knights at his beck and call," Argon said. "And his friends are also necromancers. So which side do you stand on? A murderer's? A necromancer's? Princess Mirabella witnessed Zane murder our father on the hunt, and then she was taken away, bound and gagged. Do you want Zane telling you what to do after all the crimes he has been responsible for?"

"But...you're dead," the guard said incredulously.

19

W hen the little girl distracted Kersta while she was fighting the dark knight, he swung his sword at Kersta and slammed his sword against her staff so hard, it sent it flying. Kersta didn't have a choice now. Before he could swing his sword at her and slice her in two, she whipped her cloak around and lunged for the little girl, sweeping her up in her arms and under the cloak, making them both invisible.

"My mother and sister are in danger. My uncle is hurt. My aunt and her boys ran away. Can you save us?" the girl asked.

"Aye." Kersta glanced back at the dark knight who was still swinging his sword at the air, trying to connect with Kersta's invisible body. But she was racing for her staff, grabbed it up, making it invisible, and she ran up the hill to the little girl's home with her clutched tightly in her arms. Kersta was dodging fighters, unsure if Zane's knights were fighting with the dark knights or not.

But then she saw Leogane up ahead and he shouted to Zane's knights, "You are aiding the undead, men!"

That's when her worst fears were realized. Zane's men had joined the fight against the ones battling the dark knights. She was still running up the hill as Leogane pulled the helm off a dead dark knight. "You see? He turned to ash. Kill them by stabbing them in the heart—don't ask. I have no idea why they have a heart or why it works. Or behead them. It's the only way to kill them."

She reached the little girl's mother and found her trying to stop her brother's wound from bleeding. Kersta set the girl down and switched her cloak around, then pulled out her healing pack from her pouch. "Let me do this." Kersta always wished Mexia was about when she had to deal with healing someone. *Oh*, her healing tea. She pulled out her flask. "And drink this." She handed him her flask, added herbs to a compress, and bandaged his wound. "Let's take him inside."

She noticed Leogane had finally convinced some of Zane's knights and foot soldiers to fight the dark knights instead.

Another of Zane's men shouted out to the ones who were now fighting for Argon, "What are you doing? Switching allegiances?"

"They are the undead. Vladek's a necromancer," one of Zane's knights said. And then the word began spreading.

Kersta knew what she had to do now. Unless she was needed to fight, she was taking care of the wounded. "Do you have a healer?" she asked the woman.

"Aye," the woman said. "On First Street. Mai is in the mossy green cottage at the end of the street."

"Your brother will be fine. I need to replenish my healing pack though so I can take care of others who have been wounded." Kersta replaced her healing pack and secured her flask to her belt.

"Can I show her the way?" the little girl asked.

"You should stay here and help your mother with your little sister," Kersta said, not wanting the girl to be in danger while they navigated the fighting in the streets.

"Aye, come help with your sister," her mother said, as Kersta and the woman helped move her brother into the home and onto the woman's bed.

Then Kersta was off, running toward First Street, calling out to one of Zane's knights who was fighting one of Leogane's, "The dark knights are dead, raised by the necromancer, Count Vladek!"

That gave the knights both pause.

"Behead them or strike them in the heart and that will kill them. Remove their helm afterward if you do not believe me. All you will find are ashes," Kersta said.

Then she continued to run toward the healer's cottage, the fighting between the two knights having stopped. She hoped that her words were enough to convince Zane's men to fight the necromancer's men instead.

Before she could reach the healer's cottage, she was facing two knights—one of Zane's, one of Vladek's.

Would they never get the word to all of Zane's knights to fight the real foe?

But she had a new mission, and she swept her cloak around and turned invisible, then ran down an alley and back up the hill, heading for the healer's cottage again. When she finally reached the door and knocked, there was no answer. She opened the door and peeked inside.

"Hello? Is anyone here?"

No one answered. Kersta hated taking herbs that she hadn't asked for permission to have, but she would leave coin for them. She found the herb room and was gathering what she needed, and more bandages too, when a blond-haired woman came out of another room.

"You're...you're with the others who came for Mirabella," the woman said.

"You're the woman who was serving as her maid on the

Emerald Isle of Mists?" Kersta readied her staff. The woman was on the necromancers' side, as far as she knew.

"I was forced to do Vladek's bidding. He took me hostage when I was in the countryside healing a villager who had a baby but ended up nearly losing it. I saved them both before I had to leave with Vladek. The healer, Mai, is my grandmother, though I live in the country to take care of the people out there. Vladek said he'd kill my grandmother if I didn't go willingly with him to try and convince Leogane that he shouldn't marry Princess Mirabella. It was the only reason I agreed to do it. I couldn't sacrifice my grandmother. Once the necromancer and his friends and their dark knights came here, Vladek released me, figuring I could do him no harm and I returned to see my grandmother. She was gone. I saw the fighting taking place all over the streets and I came here to grab a healing pack and more supplies to help take care of the injured. Vladek could have killed me, but he said he knew he had given me a task that was beyond my abilities and then released me instead. I've never met the princess before, and at the time, I didn't know Vladek was a necromancer, only that he was desperate to marry Mirabella before Leogane did."

Kersta opened her mouth to speak, but a man swept into the room wearing black robes, his hair long and red, his beard just as curly, steely blue eyes pinning her with a hard gaze.

Justina's eyes widened and she let out a squeak.

"A necromancer," Kersta let slip out from under her breath. At least she assumed he was one of them from the way he was dressed, and Justina seemed to be just as afraid of him.

"How do you know I'm a necromancer?"

It wasn't Vladek. One of his fellow necromancer friends. Greaves. Kersta recognized his voice when he had been speaking to Vladek in Argon's chamber.

"Greaves," Justina whispered.

Where were all the mages when Kersta desperately needed one?

In Argon's father's chamber at the castle, Mexia finally cast the spell to make Argon visible and the castle guards nearly dropped their swords. "You are...are alive," the one said.

"Aye. Are you taking the king and...uh, queen hostage?" Argon asked, not that he would allow it, but he wanted the guards to come to their senses.

"Nay. We follow you, not a false ruler who would murder his own father," the one guard asked, who Argon knew cherished his own parents.

"All right, then come with us. We will capture my brother and his friends and confine them first so they can be tried for their crimes," Argon promised.

They all headed out into the hall, Lazarion and Talamaya armed and ready for any confrontation.

But they found the halls empty, except for Listra and the older maid, scurrying out of their way.

"Where is Prince Zane and his friends?" Argon asked.

"He has joined the fight in the square, my lord. He...he said you were dead," the older woman said.

"I told ye I warned Prince Argon before his brother had him murdered so he could get safely away," Listra said.

"Aye, but Prince Zane still said Prince Argon died at the hands of assassins," the older maid said.

"What of the necromancers? Vladek and his friends?" Argon asked.

"We don't know about them," Listra said. "Only that Prince Zane led his forces out to quell the fighting in the streets."

"All right. Come on," Argon said to his allies, though the

mages remained unseen. It was a good ploy, if they came upon the necromancers and they could attack the necromancers before they could fight back. To the women, Argon said, "Find some place to go that's safe."

Then he hurried off, Talamaya and Lazarion right behind him. The mages too, most likely, though he didn't even hear their footfalls.

They went to Argon's chamber first to see if Vladek had retreated to there, but he hadn't. And Argon suspected they would have heard the mage roaring his frustration, once he learned his focusing orb was gone.

"Should we go into town to deal with your brother and persuade his knights not to follow him?" Lazarion asked.

"My friends and I will want to stay here with me to fight Vladek and his mage friends," Derek said, his voice robust, though he was still invisible.

Mexia spoke up then. "I'll stay here with Derek and the other mages."

Argon understood why she would. They needed all the mages they could get if they were to fight against three necromancers.

"We will go with you, Argon," Talamaya said.

And then the party split up—Talamaya, Lazarion, Gallant, and Argon rushing through the castle to get outside. What Argon hadn't expected was for the guards, who had intended to imprison the king and Talamaya, to go with them.

"We want the others to know we are on your side," the one guard said, and Argon was gladdened that the guards would take his side and not his brother's after what he had done.

"Aye, anyone who would ally with necromancers is not worthy of ruling us here," the other guard said.

As soon as they met more of the royal guard staff, the one guard said, "We follow Prince Argon." And he briefly explained what was going on, while Argon and his party continued toward the doors of the castle, intending to leave and join Kersta and the others in the town as quickly as they could.

"What about the necromancers?" one of the guards who was close behind Argon asked.

"Mages are dealing with them," Argon said, tossing back over his shoulder. "We can't fight the necromancers without the mages' help."

"They can't touch me," Gallant said, tapping his war hammer to his helm.

Talamaya shook her head. "They can't force you to do anything with a mind spell, but they can strike you with offensive spells that you cannot counter."

"Aye," Gallant reluctantly admitted.

As soon as they were outside the keep and in the inner bailey, two knights, who were getting ready to leave the castle grounds, saw Argon and his group of castle guards and his friends and detoured to meet up with him, both bowing their heads.

"Come with us if you want to end a murderer's rule and eliminate the necromancers' dark knights he has unleashed upon the town," Argon said.

Four boys were hurrying to bring saddled horses for Argon, Talamaya, Lazarion, and Gallant. "Per Sir Grant's orders, my lord," the one stable hand said.

Relieved to see his saddled roan, Argon mounted his horse and was glad his men were turning on his brother and aiding them. Lazarion helped Talamaya onto her saddle and then climbed into the saddle on his own borrowed horse.

Then they headed out at a gallop with the other two knights in tow, the guards running on foot, and Gallant on horseback finally catching up.

Argon just prayed that Mexia and Derek and the other

mages would have enough combined spell power to defeat Vladek and his friends. He hoped with all his heart that Kersta was safe, though he heard all the wild battling in the streets and knew the fight was not over.

"The dark knights must be beheaded or stabbed in the heart," Argon warned the fighters. "They are the undead. And Vladek intended to have our people slaughtered tonight so he would eventually rule over all."

"The bugger," Gallant said. "No necromancer will rule over me. Not over my dead body."

Everyone laughed.

"What? 'Tis true," Gallant said.

Argon and those riding with him raced toward the town and when they reached the first of the streets, they began fighting the dark knights, though several of Argon's knights paused to see him in the fight. These knights apparently hadn't gotten the word that the others in town were friends of his and to fight the dark knights.

"They are the undead," one of the knights with Argon shouted to the others.

And the word was carried forth. "Behead them! Aim your swords and pikes at their hearts! Kill them! They are undead!"

Argon saw Leogane and shouted to him, "Where is Kersta?"

"She was spreading the word about the dark knights."

"Have you seen Prince Zane?"

"Nay," Leogane said, then had to stop to fight another dark knight.

"I'm searching for Kersta—or my brother—whomever I can find first," Argon said.

"We're sticking with you," Talamaya said, and he appreciated that she, Lazarion, and Gallant were staying with him.

If they saw both Zane and Kersta in different directions, they could split forces to take care of them.

Then he heard Kersta yell, a blood-curdling scream coming from a cottage not far away. He turned his horse and raced toward the sound of her cry.

So did the others, even some of the knights.

At the cottage, Argon jumped down from his horse and yanked open the door.

Kersta was fighting a mage in long robes and a red beard, his hair whipping around his shoulders. He was casting spells at her, but she was using her staff to block them. Another woman was throwing pots and pans at the necromancer, but it didn't stop him from targeting the real threat—Kersta.

Argon had never seen anything like it. He charged forth, his sword readied. Talamaya and Lazarion were right behind him, Gallant leaping onto a table, scattering herbs and bottles of potions. It was a healer's abode, Argon realized.

Argon swung at the mage with his sword, forcing him to channel a spell cast in Argon's direction instead. The mage turned Argon's sword blazing hot, but Gallant threw his war hammer at the mage, striking him in the head at the same time Talamaya used her scepter on him, zapping him with an electric charge that stopped his heart. He fell to the floor in a dusty heap.

Argon kicked at his flaming hot sword lying on the floor, waiting to retrieve it until it was cool enough.

"That was Greaves," Kersta said, grabbing Argon and hugging him tight. "Thank the goddess you made it in time. I didn't think I could rally much more energy to fight him. What of your brother? He has sent his—" She quit speaking as two of Argon's knights came into the cottage.

"The ones we've been able to reach have switched sides," Argon said. "These men no longer fight for my brother."

"Aye, we would rather die than work for a necromancer," the

one knight said. "And if we did, he'd bring us back as the undead."

The people were shouting outside, and Kersta said, "I was gathering healing herbs and bandages for my healing pack to take care of the wounded. This is Justina, a healer, forced by Vladek to work for him to convince Leogane not to marry Mirabella. She didn't have any choice."

Talamaya nodded. "I will stay with Kersta and aid her. We'll protect each other. You and Lazarion, go take care of your brother, Argon. We know it must be done."

"I'll go help the injured also," Justina said.

"I will also stay with the women," Gallant said.

Lazarion gave Talamaya a hug and kiss, then he left with the knights and Gallant. Argon hugged Kersta to his chest. "I will find you when this is done."

"Aye, you will." She kissed him back.

And then Argon hurried after the others. Argon just had to find his brother and end his own reign of terror.

A knight rode toward Argon and he wondered if he meant to kill him. He didn't expect that everyone would turn against Zane so easily.

"My lord!" the knight called out. "Your brother has taken a transport boat out to reach the Duchess."

"Mirabella!" Argon shouted. "God's wounds!" He headed for the port, everyone following him down the streets, dodging fighters in their path—their goal, to stop Argon's brother from reaching the Duchess. Though in retrospect, Argon knew his men wouldn't let Prince Zane climb aboard.

Still, every time Argon and Lazarion had a clear shot to the harbor, dark knights engaged them. How many of these things were there?

"Go!" Argon's knights said. "We'll take care of these."

But Lazarion kept up with Argon, the two of them slashing

at dark knights who were on foot. And then they finally reached the docks. Two of the transport boats had been sunk. Another was tied up at a dock, but they had no men to help row the boat.

"You there, come with us!" Argon shouted to four men who had finished fighting dark knights.

"Prince Argon," one of the men said. "We...we didn't know you were alive."

"Aye, I am. We need to man this boat and take it to the Duchess now!"

"Aye, my lord," one of the men said.

The others didn't move to join them. But then three of Argon's knights rode up. "Prince Argon said to go now."

The men hurried to get into the boat, and Argon and Lazarion joined them while the knights cast off the lines.

Then they all began rowing, a king and a prince putting their backs into it just as hard as the rest of the men.

20

M exia wished they'd find the necromancers in the castle and fast. She was afraid Vladek and his friends had already left and were helping their dark knights in the town while here she and her mage friends were doing nothing to help. "Do you think Vladek and his friends have left already?" she whispered to Derek as they moved around the castle, invisible to everyone while searching for the necromancers.

"Possibly. But he's also sneaky. When we found him in the cemetery learning how to raise the dead, he slipped away into the night to do so and then he and his friends vanished, not owning up to what they'd done. We reported them to the headmaster, but Vladek and his friends never returned to the school to learn they were banished. We suspected he had been dabbling in the dark arts because his twin brother had died three weeks earlier from a lung ailment no one could heal."

"That's sad, but if he brought his brother back from the dead, he would not be who he had known him to be," Mexia said.

them in her invisible bubble of protection, the freeze spell covering it and dissipating. Her magical belt protected her from Salton's spell and would reflect it back to him but only for her.

Salton quickly cast a protection spell over himself. Then he turned and cast a spell at a group of the undead and a dozen were suddenly wearing the black armor of the dark knights, wielding swords.

Derek cast another spell at Vladek, but she didn't know which one. In the meantime, Mexia thought she could take care of the undead before they became hostile toward them, but now she had to concentrate on the armed knights. The other undead weren't armed with weapons or wearing protective coverings like armor, but they could still choke her and her friends, and break their concentration so that the necromancers would get the upper hand.

Vladek stretched his hand up to the sky, and she suspected he was calling on his reflecting stone to give him power, but thankfully he couldn't call on the power.

Mexia continued to concentrate on the undead, casting healing spells over them, and they began to collapse on the ground. In surprise, Vladek stared at his undead creations who were collapsing all over the graveyard and Derek hit him with another lightning bolt. It struck hard and the mage clutched at his chest, crying out in agony while the undead fell all around him, back to rest like they should have been all along. That was Mexia's greatest spell when it came to the undead, and she should have used it on the dark knights, but they had seemed so lifelike that she hadn't thought to use it before. Not until she saw them being raised from their graves.

It took Derek a few minutes before he could cast another spell, the lightning bolt taking a lot out of him.

In the meantime, Mexia continued to return the dead to rest, unable to hold her protective shield in place, while the other mages attacked and counterattacked Salton.

Vladek managed to cast a spell at Derek, this time striking him and knocking him off his feet. Mexia ran to him and checked him over. "What did he hit you with?" She couldn't heal Derek if she didn't know what Vladek had struck him with.

"My...heart," Derek said, clutching at his chest.

"No!" Mexia jumped to her feet and cast the stone spell at Vladek. He instantly turned to stone. She knew it wouldn't hold him forever, but she had to immediately stop the spell he was casting on Derek. She returned to Derek and placed her hand on his cheek and was glad to see the color returning to his face.

"Thanks, Mexia."

"Are you going to be all right?"

"Aye, in a moment."

"Okay. I need to help the others then."

She went back to healing the rest of the undead. Suddenly, Salton collapsed, and she watched to see if he was going to get back to his feet.

But Fessenwig said, "He's dead. What about Vladek?"

Mer helped Derek to his feet and Derek cast a spell breaking the statue of Vladek into a thousand pieces. "He's dead."

The rest of the undead slipped back to the ground.

Mexia stared openmouthed at the pile of rubble that had been Vladek encased in stone, then she smiled at Derek and hugged him. "I think we're going to make a great team. You didn't tell me you could destroy rock."

"I thought my lightning spell would have worked on him. But when he began squeezing my heart with his spell, I knew I wasn't going to make it unless one of you could stop him. Turning him to granite was perfect."

"What were you casting on the undead, Mexia?" Mer asked.

"A healing spell. It had worked for me before. I should have thought about it when we were dealing with the other dark knights before."

"You didn't even know they were the undead at the first, did you?" Derek asked.

"No, you're right, we didn't. What spells did you cast on Salton?" Mexia asked the other mages.

"Several spells at once," Fessenwig said. "All piled up on him. He couldn't fight both of us at once. And as long as we didn't cast something that would cancel the other's spell out— like fire and ice, we were hitting him with twice the spell power."

"Okay, that's good to know," Mexia said, though when she was fighting things, she was usually the only mage there. Now when she was with Derek, that was another situation all together.

"Let's go," Derek said, still rubbing his chest.

Mexia stopped him and put her hand on his chest. A faint glow of yellow light emanated from her hand and his chest, heating and healing it. Fessenwig grabbed his arm to steady him. Derek looked drowsy, like he was going to fall asleep. And then he began to perk up and he let out a long sigh.

"Much better, but I still feel I could take a long nap. Let's get into town. Mexia can use her healing spells on the undead, if any more are roaming around and we can find the last necro-mancer and terminate him. And then after he is eliminated, that should be the end of the rest of the undead," Derek said as they headed out on the dark road through the woods and back into town.

But they didn't see any more fighting. No more dark knights battling with their friends. And Mexia thought that might mean that the other necromancer was dead also. At least she hoped so. Then they began seeing people that had come together to fight the dark knights—Talamaya's brother and his friends, Leogane and some of his men, no sign of Lazarion, Argon, or Talamaya and Kersta though.

"Have you seen Talamaya or Kersta? Gallant?" Mexia asked Prince Grisom.

"Aye, they are healing the wounded. Gallant is watching out for them."

"Good. What about the last necromancer?"

Prince Grisom said, "Greaves is dead."

"Oh, good. We were worried about him. And Lazarion and Argon?" Mexia asked.

"They learned that Zane was attempting to go to the Duchess and board it."

"Oh, no," Mexia said.

"Argon's sailors would not allow it." Grisom glanced down one of the streets. "Talamaya and Kersta are over there."

"Talamaya! Kersta!" Mexia ran to join them, and they gave hugs all around.

"Is everyone safe?" Talamaya asked.

"Lazarion and Argon have gone after Zane, but the other necromancers are dead, and the undead put to rest," Mexia said.

"Help us to heal the injured then," Talamaya said. "You are our best healer."

That's when an old woman met up with them, giving Justina a hug and a kiss. She said to Kersta and the others, "I'm Mai, the local healer. Thanks be to thee for helping me heal the wounded. I've already heard how my granddaughter was forced to work for Vladek so that he would spare my life. I hope that the prince and princess can forgive her."

"I'm sure they will." Since Kersta could understand the dilemma Justina had faced and she knew Argon and Mirabella were good people. "I used some of your supplies."

"And you helped to kill a necromancer in my home and keep him from killing my granddaughter. Better that you and your friends met up with him than me. I wouldn't have known what to do with him. I'm off to assist some more who are injured. If you need any more of my poultices, feel free to use them." The healer inclined her head and ambled off to help others. But Justina asked for permission to join her grandmother and Talamaya gave it, even though it wasn't her place to do so.

Mexia knew Talamaya and Kersta would want to learn if Lazarion and Argon were all right, but they also had a job to do.

Kersta squeezed Mexia's hand. "Come on. We heard a group of Lazarion's knights were injured badly. This way."

"We'll help," Derek said, and he and the other mages hurried off with them.

Most mages had some healing skills so they would certainly be welcome now.

21

"Your men won't let Prince Zane on the ship," Lazarion said to Argon as they rowed out to reach the Duchess hidden by the cliffs on the peninsula. "Will they?"

"I wouldn't think so, unless somehow he convinced them he's in the right and I'm in the wrong. No matter what, I have to end this now." Then Argon changed the subject. "You're going to wed Talamaya soon, aren't you?"

"Aye. I would have done it by now if you—"

Argon sighed. "Hadn't asked the women to help me rescue my sister."

"And you and Kersta?"

Argon smiled and nodded, continuing to row his heart out.

"The tide is turning for you," Lazarion said. "I've never seen people switch their loyalties so quickly."

"All they had to do was learn that my brother killed my father and had allied with a necromancer who was planning to take over this region and others through his undead dark knight forces," Argon said, for the benefit of the men helping to row the boat out to the Duchess in case they hadn't heard the truth. The Duchess was anchored beyond the point so no one would be aware she had returned, but somehow his brother must have learned of it.

"A necromancer, you say, my lord?" one of the men rowing said.

"Three to be exact, but one of them we killed," Argon said.

"Necromancers," another of the men said, sounding aggravated.

"Your brother ordered your father murdered? By one of the ones on the hunt?" one of the men asked.

Argon's father had been a fair ruler so replacing him with Argon's murderous brother wouldn't have set well with their people.

"Princess Mirabella witnessed my brother do the deed," Argon said. "That's why he sent her away, bound and gagged."

"We didn't know," one of the men said.

"You couldn't have done anything about it. We needed to be here to take care of the necromancers and my brother," Argon said.

"It was impressive that you gathered so many men to come with you and fight for you," one of the men said.

Lazarion smiled at that, but neither he nor Argon said why he had so many men fighting for him here. Right now, Argon seemed like the good guy in all this, but if he explained how he'd taken three women and a dwarf hostage to rescue his sister and their betrotheds had come to rescue them, he knew he wouldn't be seen in a good light.

"The prince told us some foreigners were attempting to lay siege to the town. But we didn't understand it because they weren't hurting our people, just Vladek's knights," another man said. "Of course, we knew Vladek's knights were allied with Prince Zane, so we thought they were on our side also."

"Necromancers," the one man said again, shaking his head.

"Then here comes Prince Zane's knights and they began

fighting the foreigners, so we were sure the foreigners were in the wrong and Zane's and Vladek's forces were in the right," one of the men said. "No way would we have thought anything else. I've never fought the undead, let alone seen them."

They rowed forever when they saw the ship ahead. A transport boat was tied to the ship, the men still aboard, Prince Zane yelling to be brought up.

"This is Prince Argon's ship, ye bastard!" the bos'n mate called down.

"I'll have your head. Argon is dead. Let us up there. I'm in charge. 'Tis my ship."

Argon rowed all the harder to get there. All of a sudden, his men on board the ship cheered to see him coming, waving. It heartened him to know his people were behind him.

Zane turned to see him coming in another transport boat and his face turned pale. He glanced up at the sailors on the ship. "If you know what's good for you, you'll bring the boat up."

Argon realized his brother's friends weren't on the transport boat with Zane. He had abandoned them, leaving them to fend for themselves? Argon wasn't surprised at the news.

As soon as they were close enough to board Zane's boat, the men with him drew swords as if they thought to fight Argon and his men.

"The prince killed his father!" one of the men on Argon's boat shouted.

The men on Zane's boat looked at him.

"Whoever says that lies. He died in a hunting accident."

"And the reason for having our sister bound and gagged so she could be locked in a tower on the Emerald Isle of Mists?" Argon asked, still maneuvering the boat over to Zane's so he could board it. "And allying with a necromancer and his friends who are both necromancers, who had created a whole bunch of undead knights?"

The men on the boat with Zane looked at him, appearing as though they were waiting for him to deny it. But Zane looked like he couldn't believe it himself.

"Yeah, Zane, that's who you allied with. Vladek intended to take over our princedom for himself to build his empire. You weren't going to live through the night. How many of our people would he have slaughtered to have his way? We can fight this out now, or you can be returned to the castle, and you'll be given a fair trial."

"With you in charge of it?" Zane asked.

"It will be fairer than the chance you gave Father. He had no idea the treachery you had planned for him, and he didn't have any way to protect himself on the hunt. Not only that, but then you ordered your friends to assassinate me, which they failed to do. What chance did you give our sister when you forced her to be locked away in a castle tower on the Emerald Isle of Mists?"

Argon climbed into the boat Zane was on and before he could even get his footing, Zane attacked him. He wasn't surprised. His brother had already proved how ruthless he could be.

Argon fell back out of the way of the thrust of Zane's sword.

The men on the boat with Zane, moved away from him, not wanting to be injured in the fight between the two brothers.

Argon managed to unsheathe his sword and thrust it at his brother, who knocked his sword away. The sword grew hot in Argon's hands again, and he realized the necromancer must have cast a spell that had bound itself to the sword. It glowed red and he dropped it, but it was so hot, it began to burn through the boat. One of the men used his sword to hook it under the burning blade and flipped it out of the boat and into the sea, the hot blade sizzling and sinking. The other men quickly put out the fire.

That was just the distraction Zane needed and he lunged at Argon, cutting his left arm as Lazarion shouted, "Argon, here!"

Argon turned to catch Lazarion's sword just as Zane swung his own at Argon again. With a decisive move, Argon stopped him from cutting him with a clank of Lazarion's broadsword against Zane's. Then he thrust his sword at Zane, afraid the blood loss from his wound would weaken him. He wasn't positive the men would take his brother hostage if Argon couldn't decide the battle himself.

But his brother struck Lazarion's sword and he realized his brother didn't look like he'd fought with anyone. Not like Argon had. Zane had a full rowing crew also, so he hadn't wasted any energy rowing out to the ship either.

Whereas Argon had suffered several minor cuts in battle, was bruised, and his muscles were weary. He could feel his strength ebbing with the wound his brother had given him. The hate in his brother's eyes said he had every intention of killing him, when Argon had always thought they were the best of friends. Until Zane became friends with three barons' sons, all of whom were self-serving and up to no good. Argon moved toward his brother, but the rocking of the boat was making him lose his balance too.

His brother came in for the attack again and Argon parried, but this time his brother rammed into him so hard, trying to knock him down, and God's wounds, he succeeded.

Argon was on his back, scrambling to get back on his feet. Lazarion looked like he was about to leap onto the boat to save him. But Argon's honor demanded he deal with his brother on his own.

Though he was struggling to keep up his strength and driven to get to his feet, Argon's vision blurred, and he saw two of his brother trying to run him through with his sword.

The devil take it. Argon had to get to his feet. He managed to roll out of his brother's path and Zane stuck his sword into the bottom of the boat. Argon swore Zane's sword was blurring into two. Zane was still struggling to get his sword out of the oak flooring and that gave Argon the time to get to his feet, though two of the men hurried to assist him. One of the men took the time to wrap a kerchief around Argon's arm to help stop the bleeding before Zane pulled his sword free. Argon sure could have used Kersta's healing ability right about now.

His sword freed, Zane ran at him like a man possessed, determined to kill Argon. Striking at Argon over and over again, Zane forced Argon to defend himself, fall back, parry, and damn if he was seeing three of Zane now.

And then Argon heard the telltale sound of an arrow being shot—the resounding thwack. He stared at the three arrows in the center of Zane's chest, wavering, combining into two and then one. But then another followed. Zane looked up at the ship to see where the arrows were coming from. Zane wasn't falling down, only looking stunned. Another arrow met its mark. And another.

"For our father, for Argon, for me, dear brother. You can join your necromancer friends," Mirabella shouted from the Duchess.

Argon watched her, his vision darkening as he heard a splash and saw his brother floating face down in the water— dead. And then Argon heard Lazarion say, "You will survive because I would not wish to face any of the ladies' wrath should you not."

And that was the last Argon heard or saw as he was enveloped in darkness.

～

THAT NIGHT AT THE CASTLE, everyone celebrated at a feast in the great hall and the townsfolk and castle staff and guests alike joined in the meal.

It was a celebration of the return of Prince Argon who took over the treasury and was in command of the princedom, Mexia, Kersta, and Talamaya having worked on him to heal him so he could enjoy the ceremony well enough. But it was also a celebration in that he had become betrothed to Kersta.

"Though we still need my parents' approval to go through with this," she said, sitting at the high table beside him.

"They will love me," Argon reassured her, his arm still hurting like the devil. "Are you sure you do not want to stay with me for the night?"

"Nay. We are not married. Besides, this will nearly be the last chance Mexia, Talamaya, and I will have to be together at night before we are all married, sharing the same room, talking girl talk all night long."

Gallant piped up next to Talamaya, "Aye, Prince Argon. Be thankful that when you wed Kersta, she won't keep you up all night with her incessant chatter with the other women."

Talamaya sipped some of her mead. "You didn't have to come with us."

"Aye, I did. You would never have made it through half your adventures without me. Why, if I hadn't clunked that necromancer in the head with Ren at the last—"

"That was the perfect distraction," Kersta said, glancing at the kids in the hall, petting the dragonlings. The dragon parents were near the fireplace, the only place big enough for them to rest and enjoy that the children were entertaining their offspring. The male dragon had even caught fresh fish for the feast. Earlier, Kersta had shown the little girl who she'd promised to play with before fighting all the dark knights how to use a toy staff to block and protect herself and her sister.

They might even go adventuring one day just like she had done.

"What happened to Zane's friends?" Kersta asked her friends.

"They fled the town once they learned Zane had left them to face their own fate," Mirabella said. "If they are seen, they'll be arrested and brought to trial since they had observed Zane kill our father and had attempted to assassinate Argon. Several villagers witness the attack on Argon. Some had resorted to grabbing a cart and sending it down the hill to scatter Argon's assassins."

Argon smiled. "I knew they had done it on purpose to aid me." Then he frowned. "Which was another reason I had to come back to save them from my brother."

"Exactly. What about you and Leogane, Mirabella?" Kersta asked.

"He has decided he cannot live without me." Mirabella smiled at Leogane.

"'Tis true," Leogane said.

"And you feel the same way about him?" Kersta asked.

"Aye."

"What about Justina?" Kersta asked.

"Argon and I have spoken with her," Mirabella said, "and told her she was not to blame. She never tried to actually hurt me and she's a well-respected healer out in the country, though we didn't know her as Justina. She went by Tina and we'd never met her in person. We need her kind to assist our countryfolk."

"Aye, what Mirabella says is true." Argon squeezed Kersta's hand.

Kersta squeezed his hand back. "What about King Inari?"

"I've sent an envoy to speak to him"—Argon leaned back in his chair—"explaining what had happened here and wanting an explanation as to why Mirabella was locked in the tower on the

Emerald Isle of Mists. King Inari has no say in who Mirabella weds, but if Duke Leogane and King Inari want a treaty between them, that's all good."

"And you?" Kersta asked.

"I must hear back from the king concerning locking my sister in the tower. He will have to pay restitution to her and apologize. I wouldn't put it past our brother to have told the king lies and that's why King Inari incarcerated her, but I want the truth. She is owed that much," Argon said.

"I agree," Kersta said.

"I propose we take the ladies home on our ships, though I heard Prince Grisom was intending to take them home since he's returning to Damar on the morn," Lazarion said. "But I, for one, am not giving up Talamaya now until we are wed."

"I agree," Leogane said. "I hope your port can receive all our ships because if Kersta's parents agree to her marrying you in Damar, Argon, Mirabella will want to be there and so will I."

"Aye. There's plenty of room for a whole armada of ships," Talamaya said.

"I'll be traveling with all of you also," Derek said. "One last stop in Damar and then Mexia and I are returning to Albion."

Mexia agreed. "That's what I said. We just got a little side-tracked."

"Which is always the way it happens with you ladies and Gallant," Lazarion said, cocking a brow, a smile playing on his lips.

The ladies laughed.

"This time it will only be a trip home," Kersta said.

EPILOGUE

Once they arrived in the Kingdom of Damar, it was time for one celebration after another—first, King Lazarion's wedding to Talamaya and now she was a queen, still holding onto the scepter of salvation. Did that mean that by marrying Talamaya, Lazarion had won control of the scepter in the end after all? Talamaya said no to that, with a twinkle in her eye. Her mother, queen of Damar, and her twin brother, Prince Grisom, were happy for them, and glad for the alliance with his people.

And Kersta's wedding to Prince Argon was held the following night, her parents thrilled she was now a princess and had found a man they felt truly worthy of her. Her former suitors would have to find other suitable maids to wed. If any of them had gone with her on her quests, maybe the outcome would have turned out differently. Though the soothsayer Modi wouldn't have agreed. And neither would Kersta or Argon.

Prince Argon's sister, Princess Mirabella, wed Leogane the same night, Kersta insisting because as far as she was concerned, they were like sisters and would share secrets like she had with her friends Talamaya and Mexia. And oh, well, of course, Gallant.

Mexia married Prince Derek the following night and became a princess, something she'd never aspired to. A master mage, aye. A princess, nay. But she and he would run the mages school, a first for a woman, and their new ruling for admissions? Women who had an infinity for magic could test to enter the school. Even Derek's sister planned to apply and Kersta was certain she would be accepted. She was most grateful to Mexia who had helped to make that happen.

Gallant vowed to move to King Lazarion's kingdom so he could continue to watch out for Queen Talamaya, though he was still planning on taking on guild quests. It wasn't the same for him though, now that he would be doing the quests on his own like he had in the beginning. Though...a dwarf adventurer, Lila, worked for the Malaron Adventurer's Guild in King Lazarion's realm and had been on his ship since she'd done so many quests for the king in the past. Once Gallant had met her at the first of the weddings, he had expressed an interest in joining up with her on quests some time. But the dwarf turned Gallant down, not wishing for him to slow her down, or take half her quest money on a mission. Kersta suspected she'd wanted to see the dwarf from Kern who had helped the ladies with so many impossible quests.

"Come on, woman," Gallant said to Lila during the feasting as Kersta listened in, amused. "I tell ye, we fought red devil wolves, white ones, snow spirits, cyclops, mermaids, you wouldna believe all the stuff we had to do. You would be safer with me if we did the mission together."

"Finding a missing calf?" Lila scoffed.

"Aye. What if an ogre has taken it hostage? Or a goblin? You could use my fighting skills."

"I will sweet talk the ogre or goblin into turning the calf over." Lila pulled off another hunk of boar's meat to eat.

Gallant glanced in Kersta's direction. "Tell her, woman, she needs me."

Kersta winked at Lila. "If a goblin takes your food pack, Gallant is so...gallant, he will offer to share his portion of his food with you."

Lila looked at Gallant to see if that was so.

Gallant frowned at Kersta, then raised his brows at Lila. "Aye, 'tis so. The best portions too."

"That is good to know. I will think on it." Then Lila smiled at Kersta, as if she knew the truth.

Kersta wouldn't be surprised.

The dragons had turned out for the weddings in Damar, bringing their whole brood of dragonlings, which were very well mannered, considering their young age. Two of them wanted to be with Kersta during the ceremony and she realized they had imprinted on her when they were breaking out of their shells on the transport boat, though not enough that they had given up their mother and father as their parents. On the visit to Damar, they had found a dragon colony they wished to join and were settling in, though none of the companions lived there now. Since Kersta had family in Damar, she and Argon would visit from time to time and vowed to see the dragons too.

Each of the companions and their mates had contributed a mountain of gold to the dragons—or at least a start, per their request, all except for Gallant, of course. He might have been a dragon in a previous life, if he believed in such a thing.

And Prince Argon was happy to pay Gallant a substantial fee for aiding him in freeing his sister and his princedom. He also had knighted Gallant, so when the dwarf went home to the town of Kern on visits, he would have to be addressed as Sir Gallant by all his friends and family, which pleased him to no end, almost as much as earning payment for a quest.

Even Lila—though Kersta swore she was trying to appear not so—seemed impressed.

Best of all—whenever they had a chance—the ladies and Gallant planned to get together for a quest or two in one kingdom or another while visiting each other and sometimes their mates said they would join in on the danger—and the fun —too. For old time's sake. Gallant was still hopeful Lila would agree to go with them one of those times.

Kersta couldn't believe the mysterious, cloaked man from the tavern in Langdon would end up being her mate, nor had he ever thought she would be his either, but Modi was never wrong.

ACKNOWLEDGMENTS

Thanks so much to Donna Fournier and Darla Taylor for beta reading for me and finding errors that I know the fae stuck in there when I wasn't looking! You are the greatest!

AUTHOR BIO

USA Today bestselling and award-winning author **Terry Spear** has written over a hundred paranormal romance novels, young adult, and medieval Highland historical romances. Her first werewolf romance, *Heart of the Wolf*, was named a 2008 *Publishers Weekly*'s Best Book of the Year, and her subsequent titles have garnered high praise and hit the *USA Today* bestseller list. A retired officer of the U.S. Army Reserves, Terry lives in Spring, Texas, where she is working on her next werewolf romance, shapeshifting jaguars, cougar shifters, vampires, hot Highlanders, and having fun with her young adult novels, helping with her granddaughter and grandson and raising two havanese.

For more information, please visit www.terryspear.com, or follow her on Twitter, @TerrySpear.

She is also on Facebook at https://www.facebook.com/Terry-SpearParanormalRomantics. And on Wordpress at: http://terryspear.wordpress.com/

And her Wilde & Woolley Bears, award-winning teddy bears, that have found homes all over the world: www.celticbears.com

ALSO BY TERRY SPEAR

Heart of the Cougar Series:

Cougar's Mate, Book 1

Call of the Cougar, Book 2

Taming the Wild Cougar, Book 3

Covert Cougar Christmas (Novella)

Double Cougar Trouble, Book 4

Cougar Undercover, Book 5

Cougar Magic, Book 6

Cougar Halloween Mischief (Novella)

Falling for the Cougar, Book 7

Catch the Cougar (A Halloween Novella)

Cougar Christmas Calamity Book 8

You Had Me at Cougar, Book 9

Saving the White Cougar, Book 10

Heart of the Bear Series

Loving the White Bear, Book 1

Claiming the White Bear, Book 2

The Highlanders Series: Winning the Highlander's Heart, The
Accidental Highland Hero, Highland Rake, Taming the Wild

Highlander, The Highlander, Her Highland Hero, The Viking's Highland Lass, His Wild Highland Lass (novella), Vexing the Highlander (novella), My Highlander

Other historical romances: Lady Caroline & the Egotistical Earl, A Ghost of a Chance at Love

≈

Heart of the Wolf Series: Heart of the Wolf, Destiny of the Wolf, To Tempt the Wolf, Legend of the White Wolf, Seduced by the Wolf, Wolf Fever, Heart of the Highland Wolf, Dreaming of the Wolf, A SEAL in Wolf's Clothing, A Howl for a Highlander, A Highland Werewolf Wedding, A SEAL Wolf Christmas, Silence of the Wolf, Hero of a Highland Wolf, A Highland Wolf Christmas, A SEAL Wolf Hunting; A Silver Wolf Christmas, A SEAL Wolf in Too Deep, Alpha Wolf Need Not Apply, Billionaire in Wolf's Clothing, Between a Rock and a Hard Place, SEAL Wolf Undercover, Dreaming of a White Wolf Christmas, Flight of the White Wolf, All's Fair in Love and Wolf, A Billionaire Wolf for Christmas, SEAL Wolf Surrender (2019), Silver Town Wolf: Home for the Holidays (2019), Wolff Brothers: You Had Me at Wolf, Night of the Billionaire Wolf, Joy to the Wolves (Red Wolf), The Wolf Wore Plaid, Jingle Bell Wolf, Best of Both Wolves, While the Wolf's Away, Christmas Wolf Surprise, Wolf Takes the Lead

SEAL Wolves: To Tempt the Wolf, A SEAL in Wolf's Clothing, A SEAL Wolf Christmas, A SEAL Wolf Hunting, A SEAL Wolf in Too Deep, SEAL Wolf Undercover, SEAL Wolf Surrender (2019)

Silver Bros Wolves: Destiny of the Wolf, Wolf Fever, Dreaming of the Wolf, Silence of the Wolf, A Silver Wolf Christmas, Alpha Wolf Need Not Apply, Between a Rock and a Hard Place, All's Fair in Love and Wolf, Silver Town Wolf: Home for the Holidays

Wolff Brothers of Silver Town Wolff Brothers: You Had Me at Wolf

Arctic Wolves: Legend of the White Wolf, Dreaming of a White Wolf Christmas, Flight of the White Wolf, While the Wolf's Away

Billionaire Wolves: Billionaire in Wolf's Clothing, A Billionaire Wolf for Christmas, Night of the Billionaire Wolf

Highland Wolves: Heart of the Highland Wolf, A Howl for a Highlander, A Highland Werewolf Wedding, Hero of a Highland Wolf, A Highland Wolf Christmas, The Wolf Wore Plaid,

Red Wolf Series: Seduced by the Wolf, Joy to the Wolves, Best of Both Wolves,

~

Heart of the Jaguar Series: Savage Hunger, Jaguar Fever, Jaguar Hunt, Jaguar Pride, A Very Jaguar Christmas, You Had Me at Jaguar

Novella: The Witch and the Jaguar

Dawn of the Jaguar

~

Romantic Suspense: Deadly Fortunes, In the Dead of the Night, Relative Danger, Bound by Danger

~

Vampire romances: Killing the Bloodlust, Deadly Liaisons, Huntress for Hire, Forbidden Love, Vampire Redemption, Primal Desire

Vampire Novellas: Vampiric Calling, The Siren's Lure, Seducing the Huntress

~

Other Romance: Exchanging Grooms, Marriage, Las Vegas Style

~

Science Fiction Romance: Galaxy Warrior

Teen/Young Adult/Fantasy Books

The World of Fae:

The Dark Fae, Book 1

The Deadly Fae, Book 2

The Winged Fae, Book 3

The Ancient Fae, Book 4

Dragon Fae, Book 5

Hawk Fae, Book 6

Phantom Fae, Book 7

Golden Fae, Book 8

Falcon Fae, Book 9

Woodland Fae, Book 10

Angel Fae, Book 11

The World of Elf:

The Shadow Elf

Darkland Elf

Blood Moon Series:

Kiss of the Vampire

The Vampire...In My Dreams

Demon Guardian Series:

The Trouble with Demons

Demon Trouble, Too

Demon Hunter

Non-Series for Now:

www.ingramcontent.com/pod-product-compliance
Lightning Source LLC
Chambersburg PA
CBHW031320170626
46807CB00002B/500